Taking no time out for thought, he had found himself pulling Lady Cassandra into his arms, pressing the soft curves of her body against his own in a fashion designed to set his heart thudding and to send the blood rushing into his ears. And not content with merely that much havoc, he had brought his mouth down hungrily upon hers.

For her, the kiss had been total devastation. She was far too honest to pretend she had not thrilled to the feel of Godfrey's lips upon her own. And, oh dear heavens, had she actually kissed a valet back? It wasn't fair! It was too lowering! That a valet—the very term brought on a shudder—should cause her to feel this way!

Fawcett Crest Books
by Marian Devon:

M'LADY RIDES FOR A FALL

MISS ARMSTEAD WEARS BLACK GLOVES

MISS ROMNEY FLIES TOO HIGH

M'LADY
RIDES
FOR A
FALL

Marian Devon

FAWCETT CREST • NEW YORK

A Fawcett Crest Book
Published by Ballantine Books
Copyright © 1987 by Marian Pope Rettke

Library of Congress Catalog Card Number: 86-91370

ISBN 0-449-21038-3

All the characters in this book are fictitious, and any resemblance to persons living or dead is purely coincidental.

Manufactured in the United States of America

First Edition: March 1987

Chapter One

"No! No! No! Lord Devenham's voice swelled with volume and authority. His cantering horse, mistaking "no" for "whoa," firmly planted four hooves in a sudden stance that would have sent another rider over its flattened ears. But his less pliant daughter refused to take even three *no*'s for an answer. She reined in her chestnut beside the bay and tried to keep her temper. "Papa, be reasonable," Lady Cassandra said.

"Reasonable! You ask *me* to be reasonable? Perhaps then, miss, you can tell me what's reasonable about a young unmarried girl setting up her own establishment?"

Lady Cassandra Devenham sighed silently. She had hoped to catch her father in a mellow mood. The early morning sun shone down on Hampshire in the spring; it was a prospect that, according to his lordship, heaven would be hard pressed to match. They had galloped neck-or-nothing across rolling, verdant meadows, a pursuit that, though regrettably lacking in fox and hounds, his lordship ranked high in satisfaction. And to cap it off, Lord Devenham was in love. None of all this seemed to have mellowed the earl, however. He was glaring at his daughter with an expression that could have been called choleric.

Lord Devenham was rather short of stature and square of frame. His hair, grizzled and thinning, looked every day of his fifty years. His body, however, did not, a tribute to an outdoor life that compensated for his prowess as a trencherman. His complexion ordinarily tended toward the florid. Now it approached port wine. Lord Devenham did not take lightly to being crossed.

Neither did his daughter, who resembled him only in strong will. Lady Cassandra was a bit above average female height. Her hair was a russet brown. Her eyes were gray, but were equally as adept as her father's blue ones when it came to glaring. She quickly lowered her thick dark lashes to veil this tendency and counted silently to ten.

"If you'd rid yourself of your prejudices for a few moments, Papa, and look at the thing objectively, you'd see that my having my own house makes a great deal of sense." She held up a hand to stave off his rebuttal. Their horses were moving slowly side by side. "In the first place, you seem to forget that I am hardly a schoolroom miss."

"You're twenty, uh, three," he inserted.

"Twenty-four. And unmarried. And apt to remain that way."

"Fustian."

"No, Papa. It's time to stop dissembling. We both know perfectly well that the fact that your only child's a hopeless spinster played a large part in your betrothal."

"No!" he thundered, causing his mount to hesitate once more. "Well, yes, dammit, in a way I suppose it did," he qualified. "But not in the way you mean. The thing is—"

But Lady Cassandra was not yet ready to relinquish the floor. She'd spent too long marshaling her arguments. "I'm twenty-four years old, an old maid, some would say, with no aspirations toward matrimony. You are in the prime of

2

your life, about to marry a woman young enough to bear an heir for you—"

"Is that what's got your nose out of joint? Me marrying a female your own age sticks in your craw, now, does it?"

"She's not *that* young." Lady Cassandra's tongue, as it so often happened, got the jump on her good judgment. "I mean to say," she quickly amended, "that no one could think of you as old; therefore any age discrepancy seems of no consequence." Her father gave her a suspicious glance but let it go. "My only point is that your bride, regardless of her age, is entitled to run your household. And my being established there can only create friction. The servants are accustomed to looking to me for direction and will not easily break themselves of the habit."

"You're wrong, Cassie!" Lord Devenham might have just moved a chessman to his advantage. "Gwendolen don't want to run the household. Would bore her to distraction. Said so."

"But that's ridiculous!" Cassandra couldn't cloak her indignation. "She will be Lady Devenham. With all the privilege and obligation that entails. What does she expect to do, sew a fine seam and feast upon strawberries, sugar, and cream?"

"Don't be cattish, miss. Gwendolen's a Londoner. Used to a fast-paced life. Parties. Theater. Almack's. That sort of thing. It will be hard enough for her to rusticate without being saddled with a lot of domestic duties on top of it. No. She's depending on you to go on as before. And so am I." He clucked to his horse, pronouncing the subject closed. Cassandra reached across and grabbed his reins.

"But what of me, Papa?" she asked desperately. "Have you no thought of me at all?"

He looked annoyed. "Of course I have. Just said so. Nothing will be different except you'll have another woman to jaw with. Should make a pleasant change."

Lady Cassandra came close to snorting. "Even you, Papa, cannot be so besotted that you believe Mrs. Alden and I will deal well together. We couldn't be less alike."

"No, you couldn't. And that's just the point. That's why

you ain't to set up your own establishment and why I wasn't as heartless as you seem to think when I decided to bring in another young woman above you. The thing is, Cassie, you need Gwendolen as much as I do. Well,'' he added in an afterthought, ''almost as much. For you hit the nail right on the head when you said you and she ain't at all alike. Why''—his face took on a fatuous, besotted look—''the thing is, Gwendolen's a diamond of the first water. A nonpareil, in fact.''

If the implied comparison caused his daughter to flinch a bit, her parent didn't notice; he was too busy pursuing his own thoughts. ''Every young buck and blade in town was dangling after her like bees to clover, Cassie. You've never seen the like of it. And why she preferred a stodgy, countrified, old—er, middle-aged—cove like me beats all,'' he finished complacently.

Perhaps because you're rich as Croesus, his daughter offered silently.

''Anyhow''—Lord Devenham jerked himself from his self-congratulatory reverie back to practical considerations—''the point is, like I just said, you need Gwendolen. I tell you, when it comes to bewitching the male sex, nobody's more up to snuff than she is. Ain't a man alive she couldn't charm. Why it didn't take her ten minutes to have me under her spell. And not to wrap the whole thing up in clean linen, Cassie, you could use some instruction on how to deal with men. You just don't seem to know what's what. Not having had a mama since you were three must've made the difference. Always thought being a woman came naturally, but I collect it must be something you have to learn. You put coves off, Cassie, and that's a fact. You outride 'em, outshoot 'em, and worst of all, outthink 'em. And that's not the half of it. When you meet a gentleman who could be interested—and a lot would be, for you ain't all that bad-looking, actually—you just don't act the way a female should. You don't . . .'' He gestured ineffectually. ''Well, you know.''

''Simper?''

''No, dammit! Well, yes, in a way. Flirt with him, I

suppose I mean. My God, girl, you should see the way some females can write a love poem just by using their fans!"

"I have. I had a season in London, you may recall."

Cassandra's come-out, five years before, had been in 1811, the same year that George III's eldest son was named Prince Regent. Her father now considered both these events unqualified disasters.

"Don't remind me, miss. What a waste of your time and my blunt that turned out to be. But I blame myself. I shouldn't have just thrown you at your Aunt Amelia and asked her to do the job. For a bigger flat than she is can't be imagined. You needed somebody up to snuff to guide you, and that's a fact. Well, it ain't too late yet. Twenty-four's none too long in the tooth to catch a husband, and, by God, that's where Gwendolen comes in. She's agreed to help you carry the thing off. Looking forward to it, in fact. Says it will give her some amusement while she rusticates. Hadn't meant to tell you, but there it is. At least now you can see why we'll have no more nonsense about you setting up your own household."

Lady Cassandra had turned a trifle pale. She pulled her horse to a standstill once more and stared at her parent, who also reined in with obvious reluctance. "Let me get this straight, Papa. You have actually requested Mrs. Alden to launch a campaign to marry me off?" Her voice quivered with indignation.

" 'Launch a campaign'!" her parent blustered, made more uncomfortable than he would have admitted by a glimmer of tears in his daughter's eyes. "Don't talk fustian. Nothing's being launched. All Gwendolen plans to do is fill the house with company, including lots of young gentlemen friends of hers."

"A regular marriage mart?"

"If you like. Dammit, what's wrong with that? Almack's ain't got an exclusive on that sort of thing, you know. And after Gwenny attracts the company, why, then, it's up to you. At least it will be, after she's given you a few pointers. On how to dress properly. And what to talk about. All that sort of thing."

"Fan lessons?"

"No need to be pert, miss. If it comes down to learning how to peer over one of the damned things to get you settled, well, then, by George, it ain't too much to ask. For it's time you married and got such rackety notions like having your own establishment out of your head. And the main point is, there ain't an eligible man to be found in this neighborhood. But Gwendolen can supply 'em by the droves. Starting with our wedding. She's going to fill the house with company. And you'll act as hostess to her friends." Devenham tapped his horse's flank with his boot heel, effectively cutting off Cassandra's rebuttal.

As his daughter glared at his galloping back, only her horse was privy to her stated opinion: "Any gentleman friend of Gwendolen Alden is bound to be at best a mutton-headed fop—and at worst a scoundrel and a libertine!"

Several hours later, in predawn London, one of Mrs. Alden's gentlemen friends was running for his life, or at least his liberty, down the narrow streets and narrower alleys of Covent Garden. His boots, echoing hollowly as they fairly burned the paving stones, slipped suddenly on something vile and smelly, and he put a gloved hand out against the dank stone wall of an abandoned gin shop to save himself from falling. In the instant's pause, above his own gasps for breath, he heard the sound of those other boots: slower, more stolid than his own, but somehow implacable. Captain the Honorable Charles Danforth swore, shoved himself off the wall, then began to run again.

But, seasoned campaigner that he was, Captain Danforth changed his tactics. He began to rely less on speed to shake off the man tailing him and more on strategy, whipping around corners, doubling back, and climbing over walls. He even cut through the front door and out the back of a bagnio, tipping his hat to the madam as he ran, a wasted gesture since she was too far gone with gin to notice. Finally he stopped in a doorway to catch his breath and to listen. Silence. The captain congratulated himself. He'd succeeded at last in outwitting his persistent shadow.

He started off once more, this time walking at a leisurely pace and in the direction, or so he hoped, of Piccadilly. Then he heard a sharp scream of pain, followed by shouts and the thud of blows. The captain began to run again— this time toward the sounds of mayhem. But as he drew near, he paused to peer cautiously around a corner.

The man who had been following him all evening was backed into a cul-de-sac. There was just enough light now from the first faint eastern glow to make out three assailants. One of them held a knife and was crouched, waiting for an opportunity, while the other two, armed with sticks, were flailing at the cornered man who, though bleeding copiously from a cut above his eye, was managing to ward off the majority of blows with a cudgel wielded with all the ferocity and dexterity usually accorded a better class of weapon.

Captain Danforth knew the advantage of surprise. And the even greater advantage of the enemy knowing it was outnumbered. "Sabers ready! Charge!" He came roaring around the corner. "View halloo! They've gone to cover! This way, men! Follow my lead! On the double! Yoiks! Have at 'em, lads!" With a few more shouts combining battle cry with hunting exhortation, he waded into the fray. "Don't dally, lads! Won't want to miss this!" he whooped, kicking the knife with a well-aimed Hessian, then following through with a leveler that was targeted at the cutthroat's jaw. He dived for the weapon before its owner could recover and collect it. There was no contest, though. The other had taken to his heels.

Captain Danforth then turned to aid his embattled nemesis. But stripped of their backup, the other assailants were fast losing their combative appetite. It took only one uppercut to the chin to send the larger of the two crumbling to his knees, from which lowered position he began his retreat, handicapped but just as determined as the others to be on his way before the cavalry arrived.

Charles pursued the threesome to the corner, shouting

encouragement to his phantom reinforcements to urge the retreat along. Then, satisfied that the field was unquestionably his, he turned back to see how the object of the assault was faring.

The enormous, soberly dressed young man was dabbing at his forehead with a blood-soaked handkerchief. This occupied one hand. He groped within the recesses of his frock coat with the other and drew forth a barker. "Hell and damnation," Captain Danforth muttered as the pistol was leveled and pointed at his chest.

"Well, I must say"—and he was hard put not to let his tone sound quite aggrieved as he offered his own handkerchief, pristine and monogrammed, to the wounded Runner—"you're dashed late producing that cannon of yours. Where was it when you really needed it? And I do think it would be a dashed sight smarter if you Bow Street Runners were to travel around in pairs. It would save your quarry no end of trouble. I mean, it's obvious that you coves can't be too popular. Especially in this neighborhood."

"Won't argue that point, sir." The policeman applied the fresh linen to his wound. "So if you think you're up to it, we'd best take to our heels again."

"If *I'm* up to it! You're the one who's bleeding like a curst stuck pig."

For the next few minutes nothing broke the silence but the sound of running boots. Charles occupied the time by toying with the idea of ducking down an alley and disappearing. But having set his hand to the plow, so to speak, a confused sense of honor kept him from deserting the wounded Runner in a hostile neighborhood. Then, before he could subdue his conscience sufficiently to allow escape, they emerged onto a thoroughfare and the opportunity was lost forever.

They paused to pant, and Charles looked around him. "By George, you certainly are the one for doing things the hard way. You took a wrong turn back there. This is the Strand. Bow Street's that way." He jerked his thumb across his shoulder in the general direction from which they'd run. "Believe me," he said as he looked down ruefully at his splattered Hessians and their drooping golden tassels, "the next time I go on a jaunt with you, it won't be in brand-new boots. My feet will never be the same again."

The Runner dabbed his forehead once again while his companion winced for his ruined linen. "It's looking better. Your wound, I mean. Not my handkerchief. Well, let's trudge on before my feet begin to swell."

"It's only a short walk from here to St. James Square, sir. I think your new boots should take you that far," the Runner said.

"St. James? I say, I don't understand."

"That is where your friend Lord Severn lives, isn't it, sir? I really wouldn't advise you to go home to Grosvenor Square. There'll be another Runner or so waiting for you there."

Charles was brightening up. "Oh, I say. You mean you're actually letting me go?"

"What choice have I got, sir?" The arm of the law, exhausted by the battle that had raged within his conscience, spoke with martyred resignation. "I'm honor-bound to, ain't I, after you come back and saved me like you did? For you had got away scot-free and all." It was obvious that the Runner's professional pride had suffered quite a blow. "But I should point out, sir, that, even so, you ain't apt to get very far. For the hue and cry is out for you, and that's a fact. They could even be watching your friend's house, though I don't think it's all that likely. For I doubt anybody thought you'd be this hard to nab."

"Whyever not?" The aristocrat seemed affronted.

The Runner, however, refused to be diverted by the question. "So if you're flash, sir, you'll leave the country quick as possible. Only let me warn you further. As soon as it's known you've given us the slip, they'll be on the lookout for you at the ports. Frankly, sir, I wouldn't give a tuppence for your chances. And when it comes to that and they do nab you—he looked embarrassed—"I'd appreciate it if you'd make no mention of our association. I plan to say you escaped back there in the Garden when I was set upon."

"Oh, you can depend upon me to back up your story. That is, if the necessity arises."

"Oh, it will, sir. Believe me, it will," the Runner observed dampeningly. "But all the same, sir, the very best o' luck to you."

Captain the Honorable Charles Danforth extended his hand. "And to you, too, Mr., er . . ."

"Mr. Gifford, sir. Jeremy Gifford, at your service." The Runner took the proffered hand, gave it a squeeze that made the other man wince, then turned his back on his bounden duty and stolidly set off toward Bow Street.

Chapter Two

The Viscount Severn snored once, turned over, cracked an eyelid, then jerked bolt upright. "My God!" he croaked, clutching at his nightcap. "Thought you were a nightmare."

"Good morning, George," Charles Danforth said cheerfully. "I was beginning to believe you never would wake up."

"But, dammit, Charlie, what are you doing in my bed-chamber at this ungodly hour?"

"Drinking chocolate, eating light wigs, and waiting for you to finish your beauty sleep. Though to be quite honest, I was just about ready to give you a shake. Here, George, have some chocolate." The captain poured steaming liquid out of a pot decorated with blue forget-me-nots into a matching cup and then took it over to his lordship, who was glaring at him through jaundiced eyes.

"My God, Charlie, you do look like a nightmare. What the devil have you been up to?"

The captain resumed his seat by the empty fireplace, put one boot on the fender, and took a slow, deliberate sip of chocolate while his lordship crawled out of the domed bed and shrugged into a dressing gown. Then he brought his cup over and sat in the companion wing chair opposite his friend. "Out with it, Charlie. I ain't got all day, you know. I'm leaving for the country around ten."

"I know that." The captain smiled engagingly.

The viscount stared back, filled with suspicion. He'd learned to be on guard when Captain the Honorable Charles Danforth turned on the charm. Charles had a widespread reputation for being handsome. The viscount knew better. True, his friend, who topped six feet by at least an inch and had the broad shoulders, narrow hips, and well-shaped thighs to complement his height, was a fine figure of a man. But his features were not at all Byronic and his dark hair resisted his valet's best efforts to make it wave. No, Lord Severn had long ago concluded, it was charm, not looks, that Charlie had by the bucketful, with laughter at the world lurking in his deep blue eyes and an engaging grin that got him almost anything. Lord Severn braced himself to resist now, but he had very little confidence in his ability to carry the thing off.

"Where exactly did you say it was you were headed for, old man?" Charlie asked.

"Hampshire," George replied tersely. "My Uncle Devenham's wedding. Got to, you know."

"Tedious, eh? Well, cheer up, old fellow. I'm going with you."

"The devil you are! You ain't invited."

"Oh, that won't matter."

"That's what you think. Just goes to show you don't know my uncle. He may be a complete flat when it comes to clothes and such . . . My word, I can't imagine who does make his coats. His cook, most likely. But he's a high stickler when it comes to doing the proper. You don't just march into Devenham Hall without an invitation."

"That's where you're wrong, George. Happens all the time. You just ain't thought about it properly, that's all."

Lord Severn set his chocolate cup, with more force than was necessary, upon the octagonal table at his elbow. "Charlie, it's too deuced early for this sort of conversation. If you've gone queer in the attic or something overnight, please take yourself somewhere else to be it."

"No, I'm perfectly sane, George, I assure you. As a matter of fact, the old brain's ticking along even better than usual, I'd say. For a perfectly brilliant idea just came to me. Happened right after Fox brought in the chocolate and I was sitting here with nothing better to do than listen to you snore. By the by, old man, I'd think twice about marrying if I were you. That sort of racket's bound to put a female off. Oh, well, then, as I was saying, I came up with a scheme that's a stroke of genius. Mr. Gifford seemed to think I ought to go to France. But the chief drawback to that plan, as I see it, is that the Frogs do insist on speaking French. Makes a good conversation devilish hard to come by. Besides, I'm a bit short of the ready—which goes without saying since that's the reason I'm on the run. Not to mention that Mr. Gifford did point out that they'll most likely be lying in wait for me at Dover."

"Charlie," his friend said with fraying patience, "my head's beginning to ache and it's all from the strain of listening to you. Who the devil is Mr. Gifford and who's lying in wait for you and why pick Dover to do such a sap-skulled thing? And last, but certainly not least, why are you looking like something I'd as lief not identify?" He ran a disparaging eye over Charlie's filthy boots, mud-speckled pantaloons, and seam-split coat. "And ain't it enough, Charlie, that you look like the dog's dinner? By God, you smell like it, too." He wrinkled his aristocratic nose distastefully.

"Don't doubt it. Lord knows what I've splashed through. I ran around Covent Garden half the night."

"Why?" Lord Severn sounded dangerous.

"This Bow Street Runner chap—Mr. Jeremy Gifford—was after me. Most persistent cove I've ever seen. Stuck better than a hound who's whiffed a fox. Then, just when I'd finally lost him and was thinking of my breakfast and

13

my bed, three footpads jumped him and I had to go back and help.''

His rapt listener, who'd made the mistake of picking up his chocolate again and taking a substantial swallow, choked. ''Why was the Runner chasing you, for God's sake?'' George finally managed to inquire after his friend had helpfully beaten him on the back a bit.

''Old Grimes had set him on me.''

''Grimes! That cent-per-center? Don't tell me you were gudgeon enough to fall into the clutches of a moneylender! And not just any moneylender. My God, Charlie, Grimes would dish his own grandmother if she was a day late paying. If you needed money, why didn't you come to me?''

''Why, thank you, George.'' Captain Danforth appeared to be genuinely moved. ''I know you mean well, but the thing is, nothing can sour a friendship like putting the touch on a comrade. Might keep that in mind, old boy. But that's neither here nor there, actually, for I didn't borrow any brass from Grimes. Did worse than that. Signed a note for Reggie Lewison, and now he's up and vanished off the face of the earth. The rumor is he's gone to France.'' The captain's amiable face suddenly looked dangerous. ''Come to think on it, maybe I should go abroad. Wouldn't need to speak French to teach Reggie a good lesson.''

George stared incredulously. ''You mean you actually signed a note for Reggie Lewison? Lord, Charlie, and I thought you were a knowing 'un. Reggie's pockets are always to let. How could you be so mutton-headed?''

''Thought he was a gentleman,'' the other replied simply. ''It's one thing to leave a bloodsucker like Grimes up the River Tick, but it ain't at all the sort of thing a cove does to his friends. Mean to point that out to Reggie when I see him.

''But in the meantime, I'm *persona non grata* here in London and apt to stay that way till I can raise one thousand pounds.'' His companion whistled at the sum and looked rather ill. ''So the best thing to do, I decided, is to go rusticate down in Hampshire with you, George.''

The viscount chose to bypass that suggestion. "How about your father? Much as the whole thing would go against the grain with him, I expect he'd rather pay old Grimes off than to have his heir chased out of the country by the law."

"This has nothing to do with my father. I don't wish to have him involved."

George studied the mulish set of the captain's face and sighed. "Well, if you think for a minute that the news won't travel all the way to Gloucester, you give the gossipmongers too little credit."

"I don't doubt you're right. But it ain't like this coil will last forever. All I have to do is keep out of the Runners' clutches for a fortnight. Then all should be right and tight."

"A fortnight!" The viscount reverted to thinking his best friend was suffering from brain fever. "What sort of miracle's going to happen in a fortnight? Think your father's going to drop dead and let you inherit? Most unlikely. Last I heard, he was fit as any fiddle. And you surely can't be thinking Lewison will be back and make things all right. Don't know what's come over you, I swear it, Charlie. You didn't used to be a fool."

"No need to be insulting."

"Dammit, you need shaking up. Who but a complete nincompoop would go surety for Lewison?"

"What else could I do? Saved his life at Quatre Bras, you know. After a thing like that, who'd expect him to let me down? Wouldn't have been the thing to do in any case. The honor of the regiment and all that."

The viscount's head was beginning to throb in earnest. "Let me get this straight. You signed Reggie's note because *you* saved *his* life in battle? Didn't it even occur to you that the obligation's supposed to be the other way around? Charlie, you've absolutely got to stop being such a damned hero. First Reggie and now this Runner person. Saving lives is going to be the death of you."

"I'll remember that, George, if I ever chance to see you crossing the street in front of a runaway carriage. Believe me, I've learned my lesson. I'll just stroll on by. But to get back to why I'm here—''

"Do we have to? I don't think I'm going to want to hear this. You can't imagine what a sane life I lived while you were in the army."

"Not sane, George, dull. You always were a dull sort of dog. Without me for a best friend, God knows the life you would have led. But don't look so Friday-faced. Really, what I'm going to ask won't put you out at all. It's a devilish brilliant plan if I do say so myself. And if you'll stop interrupting me, I'll explain it.

"In the first place, I only need to go aground for a fort-night because the steeplechase's being run on the fifteenth. Thought even a nonsporting cove like you would know that much. I've entered Trafalgar. He's bound to win a packet for me. Especially when the word gets out that I won't be riding him. That should change the odds considerably. I'm the favorite now, of course," Charles finished modestly.

"Now just a minute. You actually believe you can lay low for two weeks and then just line up with the other riders in a steeplechase and no one will lift an eyebrow? You really have gone queer in the attic. Even if the sporting world believes you're on the Continent and bets accordingly, the law won't be that easily bamboozled. I ain't a betting man myself, but I'd lay you odds that half of Bow Street will be waiting there to nab you."

"That's where you come in."

"Oh, God!"

"You see, officially you'll be the one riding Trafalgar now." Charles plowed on through the viscount's yelp of protest. "Don't bother to fly up into the boughs, George. It ain't necessary. For, at the last minute, I mean us to make a switch. I grant you, it ain't exactly the sporting thing, but what's a chap to do? Desperate times, desperate measures. And the betting is supposedly on the horse. Why, you could probably win at that, George." There was more flattery than conviction in his voice. "Oh, well, maybe not, then." He shrugged at his friend's look of complete disgust. "But come on, George, it's the only way out of this coil. God knows, I've thought on it till my head's ready to burst and it all boils down to this: Grimes gets his money or I go to Newgate. Or to France. Talk about your Hobson's choice! Oh, I know what you're thinking. My father wouldn't let me be locked away. But frankly, I'd as lief be in prison as back at the hall listening to him prose on and on about how none of this would have happened if my older brother had lived to be his heir.'' Charles stood up suddenly. ''Well, we've wasted enough time gabbing. You need to get ready for the trip. Oh, but there is one more thing, George. Think you could stroll over to Grosvenor Square like you'd just come to call? It should throw the Runners off our scent if they think you ain't got the slightest notion where I am. And that's all I'm going to ask of you, old friend.''

''All!'' There was deep bitterness in the viscount's voice as he, too, rose.

''Well, except one more minor thing. Could you have one of your grooms pick up Trafalgar at Tattersall's and take him down to Hampshire to your uncle's stables? That part shows the real genius of my scheme. Lord Devenham's seat couldn't be more than a three- or four-hour ride from the racecourse.''

''Dammit, Charlie, try to come down from your high flights and listen to reason. We ain't going to Devenham Hall. Even if you weren't a wanted man, and even if the Runners wouldn't think to check on your friends first thing—and they ain't going to dismiss me from their minds just because I pay you a morning call. My heavens! They could be here at any minute!''

''I don't think so. That Gifford seemed a decent enough chap. I expect he'll give me a good head start.''

''All right, then. Even if they don't nab you here and even if they're too daft to figure out you've gone out of town with me—neither of which is likely—I still can't just drag you along, uninvited, to my uncle's house. Dammit, Charlie, it just ain't done.''

''Of course it is. It's done all the time. You see, George, I'm going as your valet.''

Lord Severn looked temporarily stunned. But he quickly rallied. "That is without a doubt the most addlepated, bird-witted, downright chuckle-headed suggestion I've ever heard. You couldn't possibly go as my valet."

"And why not?" asked Charles.

"Because you don't look like a valet."

"I will when I dress the part."

"No, you won't. You don't have the slightest notion of what you look like, Charlie. You probably never gave it a thought. But if I had to pick a cove out of all my acquaintances to fob off as a servant, well, you'd be the last one I'd choose. Why, dash it all, Charlie, you're a regular . . . swashbuckler! And a change of clothes ain't about to disguise that fact."

"Of course it will. Nobody ever looks at a servant. You know that."

"Other servants do."

"Well, yes, I suppose so," Charles conceded. "But even if they do find me a bit peculiar, what's that got to say to anything? Come on, George. We're only talking about two weeks. Surely I can carry the thing off for that long."

"No, you can't." The viscount spoke with unaccustomed conviction. "Even supposing the other servants don't give you away, and supposing you can skulk around and not run into any guest who knows you—and there's bound to be somebody."

"I tell you, they won't look at me."

"Even supposing all those unlikely things could happen like you've planned 'em, well, dash it, man, I'd be bound to give you away myself."

"You'd do that?" Charles was cut to the quick. "Can't believe it of you, George. Thought you were a friend."

"I don't mean I'd blow the gab on you, for heaven's sake. I just mean you don't know the first thing about valeting. And while I'm no Brummell, of course, don't pretend to be, I do pride myself on always being well-turned-out."

"Oh, you are, George. Always bang-up-to-the-nines. I've envied you, in fact."

His friend looked gratified. "Thank you. And that's my point. Chesney's the best there is, you know. Any number of coves have tried to bribe him away from me. And nobody is going to believe I sacked him and hired you."

"You can say he was called home—he does have one, I suppose?—to a dying mother's bedside or some such thing and that I'm filling in for him. That is, if anybody notices and asks, which of course they won't."

"They will! I mean to say, I depend on Chesney! Why, he's the one who invented my cravat style. The one every beau in town has copied."

"Then it's high time you got another if everybody else is wearing it. Look, George, we really can't stand here arguing about this. Are you taking me along or aren't you? If I have to go to France—or Australia—or wherever—I'd best get started." He edged toward the door, looking back pathetically at his best friend.

"Dammit, Charlie, you know I'm not going to let you do that, so quit acting out your tragedies. It's just that you shouldn't ask me to dish Chesney. I'd rather pay the entire thousand pounds you owe Grimes than part with Chesney for a fortnight. You can come along. But not as my valet." He suddenly brightened up. "Why, of course! That's the very ticket. I mean, there's no better whip in London than you are, Charlie. You can be my coachman. Why, you'll be a natural."

Captain Danforth gave him a withering look. "Use your head, George. Of course I'm a natural. So why don't you just have me ride Trafalgar down to Hampshire while I'm about it? Nobody would notice that, either, I suppose," he added with heavy sarcasm. "Why, with the steeplechase just two weeks off, I'd stick out a mile among the horses. That's the first place anybody'd look. On the other hand, nobody will expect Captain the Honorable Charles Danforth, late of the Household Brigade, to become a valet. Besides," he said, putting the final seal upon his argument, "valets sleep in the house. Why, you could even put me in your dressing room and no one would turn a hair. Now how about it, George? Do I come or not?"

Lord Severn groaned and then capitulated. "All right. You come. But just don't blame me when you come a cropper. For you're bound to be recognized. Oh, my God!" He slapped his forehead. "No! Forget the whole thing, Charlie. Dammit, now see what comes of being woken up hours before my usual time and having you sitting there like a dashed nightmare and proposing to be my valet. I got so carried away by all your narrow escapes and your cork-brained schemes that I clean forgot the main reason you can't go to Devenham Hall." He paused dramatically. "Gwendolen Alden will be there!"

"Gwenny? Gwenny Alden will be there?" Charles clapped his friend heartily on the shoulder. "By George, George, why didn't you say so before? Why, that's the best news I've heard since I put my signature on that curst note of Reggie's. Well, if Gwen's among the company, that certainly puts a different complexion on going into hiding. They don't call her the Willing Widow for nothing, you know. Oh, come on, George. No need to look so platter-faced, old boy. So what if I do plan to renew an old, fondly-remembered friendship? You don't have to worry about little Gwenny. She'd never give me away. Why, if Hampshire's as tedious as you say, George, she's going to be as glad to have me there as I am to see her." He chuckled wickedly. "I daresay that between us we should think of some ways to while away the time."

"Oh, you think so?" His lordship was carelessly studying his manicure. "Hate to put a damper on your enthusiasm, Charlie, but there's a little something about the situation you don't know. 'Little Gwenny'—or the 'Willing Widow' if you prefer—ain't going to be all that overjoyed to see you. For, as it just so happens, she's my uncle's bride."

Chapter Three

*L*ady Cassandra had spent the day settling in wedding guests. But a crisis in the kitchen had prevented her from greeting the only member of the company she really cared to see. Therefore, when evening came, she ignored her abigail's disapproval-and hurried through her toilette, then rushed off to try to catch a few minutes alone with her cousin George before they were obliged to go down to dinner.

Cassandra knocked briskly on his chamber door. It was opened by a tall, muscular servant wearing a dark coat that strained across his shoulders and left an inordinant amount of wrist exposed. Lady Cassandra found herself being appraised by a pair of lively blue eyes that held a mixture of curiosity, censure, and appreciation. She took her bearings to see if perchance she'd chosen the wrong door. "You aren't Chesney," she observed acutely.

"No, m'lady." The eyes had missed no detail of an unbecoming British net evening gown replete with satin cockleshells and branches of tamboured grape blossoms, a relic of Cassandra's distant come-out. But they suddenly recalled their place and inspected the Aubusson carpet. "Chesney was called home on an emergency. I'm taking over his duties temporarily."

"Oh, I see." She looked him up and down, puzzled by his appearance though at a loss for a reason why. She finally settled on the ill-fitting coat, a state of affairs she would not have expected her fastidious cousin to tolerate.

George was seated at the dressing table, scowling into the glass while he applied a hairbrush with dubious results. At the sight of his cousin, he leaped to his feet and broke into a smile. "Oh, I say, there you are, Cassandra. Wondered what had happened to you."

The valet watched with considerable interest as the face of the newcomer lit up, transforming her from harried hostess to pretty girl. She ran across the room to throw her arms around the viscount. "Oh, George, I am glad to see you." She sighed.

"That's all very well, but please don't crush my shirt frills," he scolded fondly. "Things are at sixes and sevens with me, don't you know. Chesney's mother's dying or some such thing. He sent his, er, cousin to take his place." He shot a darkling look at the substitute, who was studiously brushing his lordship's evening coat with a dumb, deaf, and blind expression on his face.

"George, I desperately need to talk to you." Cassandra also turned to look pointedly at the servant, who took no notice. "I need your help. I wanted to catch you when you first arrived, but what with one thing and another . . . And I don't know when I'll get the chance again."

The viscount grew apprehensive. He was truly fond of his cousin, but enough was enough. Having a spurious valet who was one jump ahead of the law was all the crisis he was presently equipped to cope with. "Oh, I say, Cassie, can't it wait? I'm nowhere near dressed for dinner and you know what a Roman your father is when it comes to punctuality."

"No, it can't wait, George. I need you to talk to Papa

for me." Lady Cassandra ignored her cousin's flinch and plowed ahead. "And the thing is, Mrs. Alden's due to arrive tomorrow. And, well, there's no sense hoping you can get Papa's attention after that."

"There's no sense hoping I can get it at any time. If you're expecting me to have some kind of influence on your father, you must be dicked in the nob. He don't like me above half, and that's a fact."

"That's not true!" Cassandra said heartily, and then backed down a bit. "Well, perhaps Papa has never precisely approved of the way you live, George. He thinks the fashionable world too frivolous entirely. But he's fast changing his mind about that sort of thing. Mrs. Alden, so I've been given to understand, is very social." She paused a moment to frown at the valet, who strove to cover a chuckle with a coughing fit. "So whereas Papa has always gone out of his way to avoid society, all that is about to change. Mrs. Alden intends him to become fashionable. That's why he particularly wanted you here. Why, you actually headed the guest list, George. He plans to consult you on how to cut a dash. How to style his hair. Which tailor to patronize. What types of carriages to drive. All that sort of thing."

If Lady Cassandra had hoped to flatter his lordship, she failed. George, in fact, barely repressed a shudder. He was beginning to feel a great deal too much sought-after. He had resumed his seat before the glass and was once more brushing his hair with disastrous results.

Her ladyship was momentarily diverted. "Don't you think you should let, er—" She glanced again at the valet, who had resumed his brushing of the coat, and lowered her voice. "What *is* his name, George?"

"Name? Oh, uh, Cha—"

"Godfrey, m'lord."

"Oh, yes. Of course. Godfrey. Forgot it for a moment. Stupid of me."

"Godfrey," Lady Cassandra commanded, "would you please stop rubbing that coat threadbare and come take charge of his lordship's hair?"

"Very well, ma'am." The valet approached the dressing table while his master eyed him warily.

Lady Cassandra got back to the matter at hand. "What I need your help with, George, is a simple thing. A matter of influence. I'd like you to tell Papa that you think it's a good idea for me to set up my own establishment."

Lord Severn gaped at his cousin via the looking glass, while his valet pushed his locks this way and that. "Why on earth would I say a maggoty thing like that? For I don't think it's a good idea, and that's a fact."

"Well, then, you can't have thought about it at all."

"That's true enough, for you just now sprung the thing on me. But I've a good notion that if I did think on it for hours, I'd come to the same conclusion. Young, unwed girls don't set up their own houses, and that's that."

Cassandra sighed with exasperation. "George, you're as bad as Papa. I didn't think I'd have to point out to you, though, that I'm no longer in the infantry. We did, after all, grow up together."

"So you're twenty-three, right?"

"Twenty-four. Last week."

"Oh, really? Should have remembered. Felicitations and all that on your natal day."

"Thank you."

"But twenty-four don't make you an ancient, exactly."

"It doesn't make me a schoolroom miss, either. I'm quite old enough, thank you, to set up independently."

"No, you ain't. And if you've got the wind up over your father's marriage, well, the thing to do is to get yourself a husband."

Lady Cassandra came within an inch of stamping her foot. "Oh, for heaven's sake, George. I didn't expect that from you, too."

"Whyever not? It's what anybody of sense would say. Can't think of why you ain't done it before now. Had some rum notion, I expect, of keeping your father comfortable. No need for that anymore. You can leave all that sort of thing up to Gwenny—up to Mrs. Alden, I mean to say."

Cassandra was once more diverted. "George," she began, then glanced at the valet and hesitated. Still, there would not be another opportunity and servants always knew everything anyhow. "Tell me about 'Gwenny'."

"Tell you what?" He looked uncomfortable.

"Oh, you know. What she's like, and all."

"You mean you ain't met her?"

"Just. She came to tea here. The only thing I was able to ascertain from that is that she's very pretty—in a rouge-pot sort of way." The hairdresser at this point had a second coughing fit that, unfortunately, drew attention to his ministrations. "My heavens, George! Whatever is he doing to your hair?"

"Oh, God!" His lordship stared into the glass, transfixed.

"I call it the 'Gladiator' style," Charles offered.

"Gladiator!" Lady Cassandra sniffed. "Well, if you ask me, Caesar just turned 'thumbs down.' George, do you really intend to go downstairs looking like that? Well, never mind. We don't have much time. Go on. Tell me about Mrs. Alden. She's all to pieces, isn't she, and is marrying Papa for his money?"

George watched glassy-eyed as his ersatz valet picked up a starched cravat and began to wind it around his throat. "I don't know about 'all to pieces.' But you can't hold it against her that she's chosen a husband who's plump in the pocket. Only sensible. It's what you should do."

"Oh, I know. I should not have said that. Don't lecture me. It's just that, well, they seem so awfully unsuited."

"That's true. But, still, the same could be said of practically every married couple that I know."

"But it's more than that. It's that people keep dropping all these hints. Implying that, well, Mrs. Alden's character isn't all it should be. Oh, botheration! Not to be missish about the thing, I've heard she's had more lovers than Harriette Wilson!"

"Glug!" The viscount choked. "Will you watch what you're doing, Cha—Godfrey. You damned near crushed my windpipe with that blasted cravat."

"Beg pardon, sir."

The viscount unwound the spoiled neck piece and flung it to the floor. The valet picked up another from a large pile of starched linen and tried again.

"Shouldn't compare your papa's bride to a courtesan, Cassie." George returned his attention to his cousin. "Not at all the thing. Gwenny—Mrs. Alden, that is—is a jolly, fun-loving type who certainly has had her share of beaux. But as for lovers, well"—he looked virtuous—"I certainly would have no way of knowing, but I expect there's more talk than truth there. I wouldn't refine too much on the gossip if I were you."

"I don't. Except that I don't want Papa to get wind of all the talk. For I'm sure he thinks he's Gwendolen's one and only—with the exception of the late Mr. Alden, of course." She broke off to exclaim, "Oh, good gracious! What's that called?" She was eyeing her cousin's cravat. "The Hangman's Fall, perhaps?"

"No, m'lady." The valet sounded just the least bit hurt. "It's called the Trône d'Amour. I can assure your ladyship that it's considered all the crack in London."

"Humph! I would quicker believe in Mrs. Alden's chastity than that. Well, now, George, how about it? You're my only male relative and my final hope. Will you speak to Papa?"

"About Mrs. Alden's reputation? My God, what do you take me for? You must think I'm suicidal."

"Don't be goosish. I'd never ask you to do a thing like that. I merely wish you to try to talk Papa around to letting me set up my own household. Please, George."

His lordship opened his mouth to protest but was diverted by the hall clock striking. "Time for dinner," he said, gazing with horror at his reflection. "Damned country hours. Hate dressing in a rush."

"Oh, dear. You're right, Papa won't countenance our being late. We'll just have to find a moment and finish our conversation later." She sighed for an opportunity now gone. "Well, come on, George. You'll have to do." But she looked her cousin up and down with some astonishment. "Really, I must say, if you're still considered a pink of the ton, which I understand you are, gentlemen's fashion has certainly undergone a change in the five years since my come-out. Actually, if I didn't know you were all the crack, George, I'd say you looked a mess."

Cassandra bent to stare across her cousin's shoulder into the looking glass to check her own tightly coiffed hairstyle. She encountered the slightly piqued blue gaze of his lordship's valet.

"I wonder if your ladyship has ever considered allowing a few tendrils to escape from bondage and curl 'round the face? It would soften your features, if I may say so, and make your ladyship look less like a governess."

Lady Cassandra gasped, opened her mouth to deliver a blistering setdown, failed to think of one quelling enough, and closed it with a snap.

"Oh, I say, we'd best hurry along." Lord Severn leaped into the breach before his cousin could recover. At the same time, he glared behind her back at his blank-faced valet. "No need to put Uncle in a taking." He proffered an arm as Charles moved quickly to open the bedchamber door.

Only when the solid oak portal had closed behind them and they had hurried some distance down the hallway did Lady Cassandra find her tongue. "George, that—that—Godfrey person is without a doubt the most—most—ramshackled excuse for a valet I've ever seen!"

"Oh, do you think so? I rather like him," her cousin replied heartily.

But somehow the martyred expression on the face of the erstwhile Bond Street beau made a hollow mockery of his words.

Chapter Four

*The only way to cope with a day that included the arrival of Lord Devenham's bride was to get away from it all in the early morning and to allow fresh air and exercise to do whatever they could to provide emotional equilibrium. Therefore Lady Cassandra was cantering across a meadow soon after sunrise when she spied the other horse.

It was big. It was white. It was moving at an incredible speed. And it was being ridden by a nonesuch.

The man on horseback was deeply preoccupied. When he finally did notice the approach of another rider, he quickly swerved his horse in an oblique direction. But Lady Cassandra had no intention of being avoided. She applied her spurs.

The rider tried to pretend he was not aware of her pursuit. He nudged his horse into an even greater effort. Lady Cassandra increased her speed enough to maintain their equidistance while she seized the opportunity to study the big white stallion.

He was magnificent. His huge flanks moved powerfully, without effort. So lightly did his hooves touch the meadow grass that he appeared to skim across the dew-soaked turf. His coat was glossy. His neck arched with pride. All in all, Cassandra decided, the stallion was the most magnificent horse she'd ever seen, save one. She cupped her hands around her mouth and whooped, "You there! Wait up!"

She drew abreast with the other rider and pointed with her whip to a grove up ahead. "I'll race you. To those trees there."

The rider looked surprised, then shrugged and grinned. "Say when."

"When!" Lady Cassandra shouted, and dug in her heels. She leaned low over her chestnut's neck as the animal responded. Her high-crown hat went sailing off behind her and the wind whipped through her hair. She was riding the original Pegasus. She was flying. She was invincible. But the big white horse was keeping pace. They were only yards away from the clump of poplars when Cassandra shouted "Now!" and gave her horse the lightest of flicks with her riding crop. The gallant beast responded and pulled away. Lady Cassandra arrived at the grove a full length ahead of the snow-white stallion. Flushed and triumphant, she turned to face the man she'd just defeated.

"I knew you'd look much better with your hair loosened about your face," her cousin's valet said.

"Don't be impudent!"

"Beg pardon, ma'am. Being too quick to notice the gentry's appearance is a professional hazard, I'm afraid." Charles's face was decorously composed, but his eyes twinkled disrespectfully. "I just thought you might care to store away the observation for future reference."

Lady Cassandra mentally kicked herself for having encouraged such shocking familiarity by challenging a servant to a race. Bent on outfacing this upstart who obviously did not know his place, she gave him a chilling look. "When I saw you out riding, Godfrey, I assumed you were Lord Severn."

"I see. Well, we're often mistaken for one another, m'lady."

The absurdity of this statement, coming as it did from the dark-haired man who dwarfed her fair-haired cousin by a head, who was coatless and clad in black knee smalls and low-cut leather shoes, a sartorial solecism unimaginable in the viscount, put Lady Cassandra even further out of countenance. "What I mean to say is, I looked only at the horse."

"He is rather marvelous, isn't he?" The valet patted Trafalgar's neck.

"Yes, indeed. Almost as marvelous as this animal." Not to be outdone, her ladyship gave Pegasus a fond pat.

There was a momentary glitter in the man's blue eyes, but his "Why, thank you, m'lady" was subservient to a fault.

"I must say that George is certainly improving as a judge of horseflesh." Cassandra clucked at her mount and turned it toward home. The valet fell in beside her.

"Begging your pardon, ma'am, but Lord Severn did not choose this horse."

"I should have known. Who did?"

"I did, m'lady."

"You did? How peculiar. Perhaps his coachman should help him dress."

The valet grinned. "Actually, the matter was of no concern to his lordship, ma'am. Trafalgar here is mine."

"Yours? He can't be yours."

"Not if you say so, ma'am. Oh, by the by. You're forgetting your hat. Shall I ride back to fetch it?"

"No, I'll go myself." As the valet turned to follow, she added in a dismissive tone, "You must have duties back at the hall. I doubt his lordship can manage his Trône d'Amour without you. By the by, does he know you're out riding whoever's horse?"

"Well, no, not precisely, your ladyship. I didn't like to wake him up to inform him of it."

She stared at the servant suspiciously. Every instinct in her screamed that he was laughing at her, but his face remained decorously impassive. "I must say," she finally observed as they rode side by side, "you are a surprisingly accomplished horseman for a valet."

"Thank you, m'lady."

"In fact, come to think on it, I don't believe I ever saw any other valet ride at all."

"Begging your pardon, ma'am, but would you mind not saying v-a-l-e-t in front of Trafalgar here? You see, I've never told him how I earn a living. Might put him off his stride. Trafalgar's a very aristocratic horse, your ladyship. Bit of a snob, in fact. I'm sure he thinks I'm one of the nobs."

"You're roasting me, aren't you," Cassandra observed calmly. "Well, I would ask how a valet learned to be a bruising rider, but I collect I'd only get some Banbury tale for an answer." She watched him analytically as he dismounted to retrieve her hat. "But I am sure of one thing. You're much more at home in the saddle than you are with valeting. In fact, I should think you're more at home doing almost anything other than valeting. Tell me, did my cousin lose a wager? That's the only reason I can think of for replacing Chesney with you."

He was dusting off her hat by rotating it against his knee smalls. "If you're casting aspersions upon my professional abilities, ma'am, well, I must say I'm crushed you feel that way, for I was just about to apply for the post of your majordomo."

"My what? Surely you're funning again."

"Oh, no, your ladyship. I'm ever so serious."

"Well, then, I'm compelled to tell you that we've absolutely no intention of replacing Parker, who has been with us forever."

"Oh, but I didn't mean here at the hall, ma'am. I meant at your new establishment."

Lady Cassandra gave him a hard look. "As every *good* servant knows, Godfrey, it is customary when overhearing a private conversation to forget that the conversation ever happened."

He sighed a heavy sigh. "Are you saying, ma'am, that I'm not qualified for the post of butler?"

"That's too obvious to require saying. But in this case it's merely academic. There is no post. Nor is there likely to be."

"Begging your ladyship's pardon, but I venture to suggest that the future Lady Devenham will want you out of the hall in no time. For Gwe—er, Mrs. Alden—is not the type to tolerate being cast in the shade by an attractive female. Especially by a younger, attractive female."

"How on earth would you know a thing like that?"

"I forget," he answered virtuously.

Cassandra quite failed to look suitably past or through the valet, and was once more reminded that, if you could ignore for an instant the fact that he was a servant, Godfrey was a fine figure of a man. The seed of suspicion began to sprout. "Are you acquainted, then, with Mrs. Alden?"

His eyebrows rose. "Begging your pardon, ma'am, how could I be? It's like you mentioned before. A lot of things get said in front of servants that go in one ear and out the other. And somehow I've been left with a bit more than just an impression that Mrs. Alden doesn't care for the company of attractive women."

"If for some strange reason, Godfrey, you are trying to flatter me into hiring you, don't bother. The thing won't wash. I'm well aware that I'm no beauty, nor have I the desire to be."

"Now there you've hit the nail on the head, and that's a fact, ma'am. For it's plain as a pikestaff you don't wish to be thought attractive. Whereas most females I've had the occasion to observe manage, by all sorts of artifice, to foist themselves off as beauties when they ain't, you do just the opposite. You go out of your way to make yourself look plain, not seeming to care a fig for what you wear or how your hair's done. While the fact is, when you forget to be so starchy, like when you were racing me back there with your eyes sparkling and the wind whipping through your hair—well, m'lady, if you weren't a beauty then, you were next door to one, and that's a fact."

"That will do, Godfrey!" she snapped. "I've little use for Spanish coin."

"No, ma'am." He cast his eyes down meekly.

They rode without speaking for a while, a strained silence on Lady Cassandra's part. Her companion, on the other hand, seemed quite at ease, whistling under his breath and occasionally glancing her way out of the corner of his eye. She caught one such look and blurted out, "You're Irish, aren't you?"

He laughed aloud. "Oh, no, your ladyship. And what I was saying wasn't blarney but God's own truth. And before you get back up on your high ropes again and remind me that I never did actually hear the conversation I overheard, I'll admit I'm curious as to why you seem so dead set against marrying. What I mean to say is, it's the gentry's time-honored way out of difficult situations. Like the one staring your ladyship in the face."

"It's the time-honored way to leap from the frying pan into the fire," Cassandra answered.

"Well, yes, I suppose that is one way of viewing it. You're not exactly a romantic, are you, ma'am?"

"I see nothing romantic about placing oneself on the marriage mart. *Mercenary* would seem the better term."

"Oh, well now. I was wrong. You *are* a romantic. Waiting for someone to ride up on a white charger, then, are you?" As if on cue, his own stallion arched its neck and whinnied. The valet broke into an impish grin.

"Indeed, I am not." Lady Cassandra's frosty stare almost froze him in the saddle. "To satisfy your impudent curiosity—though I should do far better to ignore it—my only interest when a man comes riding up on any color horse would be the animal. What I long to do, if you must know, is to establish my own horse farm."

"You want to breed horses?" He looked at her doubtfully. "Well, ma'am, horses most likely prove more satisfactory than children in the long run, but still and all, it does seem pretty much a waste. And I can certainly understand why your father has taken a stand against the whole idea. You must admit it's a bit eccentric for a female. Don't you think you could possibly manage both? Horses and children aren't mutually exclusive that I ever heard."

"What I think, Godfrey, is that this conversation has gone quite far enough. And that you should concern yourself with your employer's affairs, not mine. And speaking of that, I should think Lord Severn must be wondering by now what's become of you."

"Thank you, your ladyship, for reminding me." The valet pulled his forelock. "I almost forgot my duty in the pleasure of my ride. I'd best hurry on ahead. Wouldn't do for the two of us to arrive back at the stables together."

"Whyever not?" Lady Cassandra inquired in her most toplofty tone.

"Well, you know how tongues can wag."

"If you're implying what I think you are, you flatter yourself, Godfrey. I assure you, no one would wag a tongue about a servant and myself."

"Well, of course, you could be right, m'lady. At least we both know that's as it should be. But, forgive me, being of a lower class, I possibly know the way of the world a great deal better than your ladyship ever can. And given the most trivial incident to work on—like the lady of the manor out riding in the early morning with her cousin's valet—you'd be amazed how tongues can be set awagging till the most innocent encounter is blown full-scale into a clandestine rendezvous."

"Fustian! None of my servants will think anything of the kind. They know me too well."

"No doubt you're right, ma'am. Just the same, I'll not have it on my conscience to furnish grist for the gossip-monger's mill. The decision's entirely up to you." He suddenly dug his heels into his horse's flanks and the stallion gathered its legs in a burst of speed. "So catch me if you can!" the valet shouted back across his shoulder.

Lady Cassandra's sporting blood was up. The chestnut, too, seemed spoiling for another race. Indeed, the two of them had instantly reacted to the challenge of the stallion's speeding hooves and were in hot pursuit when her ladyship had second thoughts and reined in to a decorous trot. It wasn't the increasing unlikelihood of overtaking the white horse that had put her off, though Cassandra watched its accelerated pace with an awed expression. It was the uneasy feeling that her cousin's impudent valet had just spoken some home truths.

For no matter how far above reproach her own reputation might have been up to this very minute, an instinct told Cassandra that any female of any age or class, whether schoolroom miss or crone, duchess or kitchen maid, who spent time alone in the company of that particular gentleman's gentleman would send eyebrows soaring and whispers traveling at the speed of light. He simply had that sort of aura. Indeed, the would-be horse breeder reflected, the valet exuded masculinity more flagrantly than his stallion did. He had made her more conscious of being female than any man she'd ever met.

Not that she placed undue significance on his forwardness. She was astute enough to recognize that dalliance was his second nature. And to realize that if she'd given Godfrey an inch, a mile wouldn't have begun to be his limit. It was obvious that he was ready to ride neck-or-nothing over all class barriers. Which made her wonder further if this sort of dalliance was something less than a novelty with Godfrey. And that made her wonder even further still just how he seemed to know so much about Mrs. Alden. Was it true, as he'd implied, that all his information about the widow had come to him secondhand?

She jerked herself from this reverie with a mental scolding for such unworthy thoughts. Her father had been right. She was becoming cattish. She was simply jealous of Mrs. Alden for usurping her position, and that was that.

Cassandra impulsively gave the left rein a tug and turned her horse away from the direction of the stables. She'd gallop awhile and clear all such unfounded, unworthy, unjust imaginings from her mind before she was called upon to play hostess to her father's bride.

And so the extra few minutes' delay in her arrival at the stables was dedicated to this worthy cause and had nothing whatsoever to do with putting more time and distance be-tween herself and a certain upstart valet who hadn't the slightest notion of how to keep his place.

Chapter Five

Viscount Severn was a man of honor. No matter that he had been more than a trifle castaway the previous evening after drinking port when he'd promised Cassandra to speak to her old horror of a father. No matter that the thought now crossed his mind that his cousin had taken clear advantage of his mellowness to extract the promise to beard the old behemoth in his den. The fact remained that he had agreed to do so. And the word of a gentleman in any condition was his bond. So with a face set not unlike that of a French aristo riding in a tumbril (though rather less well groomed than one of those poor unfortunates), George left his room early in the morning, the clock barely having struck the hour of ten. He intended to seek out Lord Devenham before he lost his nerve and before Charles could return from wherever the devil he'd disappeared to and make the bad matter of his appearance even worse.

The look Lord Devenham gave George as the viscount timidly obeyed a barked summons to come in in no way augered the success of his diplomatic mission. It was not warm and cordial. Indeed, impatience was writ largest upon the earl's face. Devenham, too, had yielded while in his cups to Cassandra's plea to have a word with his nephew on a matter of importance. He was also regretting his compliance.

For he had other things weighing upon his mind. The arrival of his bride was, naturally, the most pressing. But there were numerous other matters that took precedence over jawing with that young ass George. Come to think on it, any matter took precedence over that.

"Well?" The earl turned away from the library window that commanded a sweeping view of the carriage drive. He fastened a jaundiced eye on his nephew. "Cassie said you had to talk to me. Damn bad timing, I don't mind telling you. Gwenny's due any minute." He gestured toward a chair, then plopped himself down in one that put them vis-à-vis across the hearth. "Go on. Get to it."

George swallowed hard and longed for the decanter that had gotten him into this mess. He thought fleetingly of suggesting that his uncle ring for similar refreshment, then prudently decided that it would never do. He would have liked a different setting for their chat. Rows and rows of books were decidedly off-putting. Nor did the dark paneling and vast proportions of his uncle's library help to establish a cozy camaraderie.

But Lord Devenham did not care two hoots for cozy camaraderie. He had settled on the library for one reason alone. He could watch for Gwenny. And even as George cleared his throat to jog his thoughts, the earl leaped up out of his leather chair to race to the front window. "Blast! Thought I heard a carriage," he muttered as he watched an empty horse cart in the distance rattle off the carriage drive away from the house and toward the barns.

"Well, do get on with it, George." He collapsed once more into his chair and drummed its arm with impatient fingers.

"Harrumph!" George's throat once more tried to jolt his brain. "It's about Cassandra," he finally managed. "Have to speak to you, don't you know. I mean to say"—he began to put it all together—"I'd like us to talk about Cassandra, sir."

"You would? Whatever the devil for? Deuced fine gel, and all of that, of course. But she don't make for good conversation at any time. And just now when Gwenny's due—"

The mere mention of the name served as the earl's catalyst. He leaped up once more and again hurried to the window. The prospect presented a pleasing vista of green lawn and leafy trees. It yielded numerous peacocks, three gardeners at work, and, in the distance, a pair of deer, but still no carriage. "Blast!" Devenham muttered repetitiously, and reluctantly dragged himself back to the leather chair. "Well, get on with it, George. What did you want to say about my daughter?"

"Well, sir." The viscount's neckcloth had been in dire straits from the beginning. Now his tugging on it tolled its death knell. "The thing is, Cassandra insisted that I speak to you. I thought myself it was damned poor timing. What with you expecting Gwenny—Mrs. Alden, I mean to say." George was rather proud of this stroke of diplomacy and began to warm slightly to his work. "But you know how it is with women, sir. Once they made their minds up to a thing. Cassie said I mustn't wait. She said that when Gwe—Mrs. Alden did arrive, you'd never have a spare moment to give a thought to her. That is to say, to Cassie's future. And that's why she said I mustn't wait but should speak to you right away." George wiped his perspiring brow with a handkerchief that was none too fresh. Damn Charlie, anyhow. Chesney would have put a replacement into his coat. But still and all, he thought, things weren't going too badly now. At least he'd captured Devenham's attention.

Indeed, his uncle's blue gaze was now riveted on him with disconcerting intensity. If he still listened for carriage wheels, he hid it well.

"You mean to tell me, George, that you're here to talk about my Cassie's future?"

"Yes, sir." Well, at least they'd gotten that point cleared

up. The viscount drew a deep breath and prepared to forge ahead.

"Well, I'm damned." His uncle leaped into the breach before George's breath could be exhaled. "Damned and dashed. I'd no idea the wind was blowing from that direction."

"You didn't, sir?" The viscount was a bit bemused. He'd no idea the wind was blowing at all. Or just what such a climatic condition had to say to anything, when it came to that. "You see, sir," he said, trying to get the conversation back on track, "what with your own marriage coming up, and the prospect of having two women living in the same household, which you must admit most likely would be a disaster—almost always is, you know—Cassandra feels it's best that she—"

"Why, the sly puss!" Lord Devenham slapped his buck-skin-clad knee. "All that talk about setting up her own establishment. Should have known she was just trying to soften me up. Probably thought I'd cut up rough. And I must admit it's knocked the props out from under me."

"You weren't any more surprised than I was, sir. Couldn't believe it at all at first. But it does seem to be what Cassandra wants."

Lord Devenham gazed at his nephew with a look that was almost approving. In fact, compared to the way he had been wont to gaze at his older sister's child, it *was* approving. "That was damned well said, George. I admire your modesty, lad. But back to Cassie . . ." He paused and contemplatively scratched the side of his nose. "Like I just said, this all comes as a bit of a surprise. And that's not to go quite as far as I might have done and say it's a downright shock. Of course I know the gel's always been fond of you. But I never expected it to go quite this far."

"I was a bit surprised myself when she insisted that I be the one to speak to you."

"Well"—the earl frowned—"don't see why. Of course you'd be the one to do it. Only proper thing."

"You don't say so. And I thought it would be a waste of time. Thought Cassandra herself would have more influence. Told her so. But she insisted. Fairly pushed me into it, if you must know."

"Hmmm. Did she now? Well, I suppose the gel is feeling a bit desperate. After all, it's been five years since her come-out. I suppose you don't mind she's a trifle long in the tooth?"

"Mind? Why should I mind? When it comes to that, she's six months younger than I am," George replied.

For the second time in both the last five minutes and the viscount's lifetime, Devenham bent a look of approval on George. "That's damned well said, too, m'boy. And, b'gad, if this is what Cassie wants, I'll not stand in the way. Won't give you Spanish coin and pretend that it's what I dreamed of for her five years ago. But then that's not to say it ain't all for the best. Mustn't overlook the matter of the title. That speaks for something in itself. Pretty plump in the pocket, too, ain't you, George?"

"Well, yes, in a manner of speaking, I suppose I am." If George thought the question both beside the point and in rather dubious taste, he was too polite, or too craven, to say so. "But back to Cassandra—"

"Well, as you probably already know, the fortune her grandfather left her ain't really handsome. Still, I'd call it rather better than a competency. You do realize my own affairs have taken on a new complexion now that I'm remarrying." Devenham suddenly turned pink. "I could still produce an heir, you see."

"Yes, sir. That, er, probability is one reason that Cassie feels—"

"Well, it does her credit." Lord Devenham's mind had suddenly reverted to carriage wheels. He went to the window once more and leaned outside. The peacocks had increased in number. The gardeners were down to two. The deer were no longer to be seen. Otherwise, the view remained the same.

"There is one other thing, George, that I almost forgot." Lord Devenham resumed his seat along with the conversation. "Don't mean to throw a rub in my daughter's way, lad, but this house party makes the whole thing rather awkward. For I've already spoken with Mrs. Alden about Cassandra's future. Never occurred to me, you see, that the gel would take the bit in her own teeth this way. I tell you, boy, trying to figure women is a complete waste of time. But since I have confided in Gwenny the way I did, and since she wants to do something to help Cassie . . . Well, to be blunt, George, Gwenny plans to bring some suitors down from London with her. And, well, now, since she's so eager to help—wants to get into the way of being a proper mama-in-law, was how she put it . . .'' His eyes misted over. ''Well, now, I don't quite have the heart to tell her that she's troubled herself for nothing. So if you don't mind, George, we'll just not say anything about this new development until after my own wedding. It will be out little secret, eh?'' He gave his nephew a knowing wink.

''Oh, you can depend on me, sir.'' George spoke heartily but stopped just short of winking back.

''Besides,'' the earl continued, ''an announcement could be premature. Who knows? Why, Cassandra's likely to fall head over heels in love with one of those coves that Mrs. Alden will bring.'' And for just a moment Lord Devenham allowed himself a spark of hope. But then he quickly snuffed it. Somehow it seemed unworthy. There were depths to his nephew that he had somehow failed to plumb. Certainly nothing became the young man like his modesty. ''No, no, George''—the earl was at pains to sound reassuring—''I'm only funning. If Cassie's made up her mind, well, you can rest assured she ain't likely to be changing it. The gel's not fickle. Oh, I say!''

This time there could be no mistaking the sound of carriage wheels. Lord Devenham leaped from his chair again. In his rush to gain the window, he collided with a pole screen and sent it careening across the room. ''She's here!'' he whooped joyously as the viscount politely rose to his feet and ambled over to join him. ''It's Gwenny, George! By gad, it is at last! My little Gwenny's here!''

Gwendolen Alden, who was being handed out of her carriage by a dandy in his middle years, gazed at the hall with satisfaction. True, it lacked the grandeur and antiquity of more noble piles. Nor was there a portico to add distinction or a break in the austere façade. The house was, in fact, a monotonous rectangular block. But it was capped by a hipped roof, lit by dormer windows, punctuated by massive chimney stacks, and surmounted by an octagonal cupola. The effect, she had concluded on her previous visit and now confirmed, was most impressive; the sight a fitting climax to a journey that had meandered through three miles of park. All in all, Mrs. Alden was more than satisfied with her conquest.

For the widow was overripe and knew it. It was taking more and more of her dresser's art these days to conceal the tiny lines forming near the large blue eyes and to bring the rosy bloom back to her cheeks. Thank goodness, her cornsilk hair had not lost its sheen. But her ample figure now required all of her willpower and Lord Byron's regimen of biscuits and water to keep within the confines of "voluptuous" and not spill over into "fat."

A realist, Mrs. Alden knew she had captured Devenham in the nick of time. And she congratulated herself on the conquest. True, he was a dull sort of dog with an overfondness for rustication. But she would soon wean him away from the rural life. Or, better still, after a decent interval they could go their separate ways, she back to town to take her new place in society as a countess, he to join the hunts—or whatever diversions broke the monotony of country life.

There was nothing forced about the cheerful smile Mrs. Alden gave in response to his lordship's welcoming whoop. She was fond of Devenham. It was easy enough to be fond of any man who doted on one and had ten thousand a year to boot. So when he dashed outside to greet her, she returned his bear hug with enthusiasm and presented her traveling companion almost as an afterthought.

Lord Devenham's reaction to this introduction was disappointment. He had rather expected young men by the droves. Instead, his daughter's suitors had come singly, not by battalions, and the one wasn't exactly prepossessing when it came to that.

For when you got past the enormous boutonniere, the outsized lapels, the pinched-in waist of the bright blue coat, the gleaming fob, the quizzing glass, and all the other affectations that spoke of youth, one suspected that the artfully swept Brutus hairstyle concealed a bald spot and wondered if the ramrod-straight figure did not owe a bit of its trimness to a corset, which was occasionally betrayed by a tiny squeak. Indeed, Devenham concluded as he welcomed Mr. Plumb Davies to his house, the gentleman was much nearer his own age than Cassandra's. But any twinge of disappointment he might once have felt about the dearth of suitors for his daughter simply died aborning. For it really did not make a penny's worth of difference after his talk with George. Only one thing mattered now. Gwenny was here!

Within the hall, Cassandra had seized the opportunity—tactfully disguised as allowing her father to greet his fiancée in private—to seek out George before the press of hostess duties made a private word impossible. She found her cousin still in the library, and at the sight of him, her spirits sank.

Lord Severn was sprawled limply in the same wing chair he'd occupied during his interview with Lord Devenham. And he looked for all the world like someone who had just taken a dagger in the heart. Except that his eyes, while glassy, still held a glimmer of disbelief.

Even in the midst of her own despair at the apparent failure of her cousin's mission, Cassandra spared a moment to be touched by George's attitude. Given his reluctance to plead her cause, Cassandra had not expected him to be quite so crushed.

"Don't look so Friday-faced, George dear," she said gently as she sank down into her father's chair. "I'm sure you did your best. And I thank you for it. I never really had much hope that you could change Papa's mind. He's hopelessly old-fashioned. Doesn't even know we're in the nineteenth century. So I didn't really expect him to allow me to set up my own household. Still, it was worth a try.

It was barely possible that he might listen to you, another man. What exactly did he say, George?''

"Glug!'' George tried speech and choked.

"That bad, eh? Oh, dear. I should have known. Really, George, I didn't stop to think that I was letting you in for one of Papa's famous scolds. Cut up rough, then, did he?''

The viscount shook his head violently.

"Oh, you don't have to wrap the thing in clean linen for me, George. I know all too well what Papa's like when he gets into a taking. I'm just surprised I didn't hear the roar all the way downstairs in the kitchen. Oh, I am sorry. Please forgive me. I should never have badgered you into such an unpleasant interview. Really, George, you look quite shaken. What a terrible tongue-lashing you must have had.''

"No, no!'' The viscount found enough voice to croak. "You've got the whole thing backwards, Cassie. Your father was the soul of affability.''

"Papa?''

"Oh, yes. In fact, I've never seen him quite so cordial.''

"Papa? Cordial? Really, George, you're making no sense whatsoever, sitting there looking like someone sentenced to the Tyburn tree and speaking of Papa's affability. What exactly *did* my father say?''

"Oh, my God, Cassie. You surely can't expect me to remember all of that. There was a whole lot of rattling on about pounds per annum and his hopes for an heir and keeping the whole thing secret from Gwenny for a while. But the really important thing was—'' He choked suddenly and his eyes protruded, as if from the tightening of a noose.

"Yes, yes,'' his alarmed cousin prodded, "the important thing was what, George?''

Lord Severn bent his anguished gaze fully on his cousin's face. "My God, Cassandra,'' he whispered, "your father wished us happy.''

Chapter Six

*Breeding will tell. Centuries of Lady Devenhams re-*called Cassandra to her duty as chatelaine—temporarily, anyhow—of the manor. Squelching an unworthy impulse to berate her cousin for botching his assignment, she patted him reassuringly instead. "Don't worry, George. We'll work out something. I quite refuse to marry you. Actually, though," she added thoughtfully, "maybe this is a fortunate misunderstanding after all." And she took a moment to develop this odd reasoning aloud for both their benefits before she left George to dash up the backstairs in the hope of arriving before the guests.

But she was foiled by a procession toiling in front of her. Four footmen, directed by an unencumbered butler, staggered under the weight of Mrs. Alden's luggage. There was no doubt that the lady had come to stay. Cassandra felt her heart sink as she fell in behind the baggage train.

And if Mrs. Alden's luggage had had such a lowering effect, it was nothing compared to the lady herself, who was now strolling down the hall in Cassandra's direction and clinging possessively to Lord Devenham's arm. Cassandra had not imagined her father capable of looking so besotted. Still, she acknowledged, everything about the widow was designed to produce just that effect.

She was dressed in the height of fashion. Her pale blue carriage dress was completely plain until it reached a hemline enlivened with crepe puffs of a deeper, richer blue. Her corn-colored hair peeked out from under a Parisian bonnet with a crown of moderate height. A blue velvet reticule edged with silk trimming and adorned with tassels completed the modish look. Mrs. Alden might have stepped right off the page of an Ackermann costume plate.

As the widow greeted her with affected delight, Cassandra blushed for her own outmoded riding costume and wind-mussed hair. To her chagrin, she began mumbling excuses for her appearance—a crisis in the kitchen had not left her time to change—while Mrs. Alden planted a light, cool kiss upon her cheek, then turned to present her guest.

Cassandra was being appraised by a pair of knowing eyes. She guessed that Mr. Davies could barely restrain himself from employing his quizzing glass, so intently did he peruse her. Feeling more gauche than ever under such scrutiny and suddenly recalling that she undoubtedly smelled of horse (an aroma her father had once preferred to French perfume), Cassandra decided that the situation only needed the added presence of Godfrey to push her embarrassment well beyond the pale.

For the valet had chosen just that moment to saunter down the hall from the back stairway, his arms piled high with his master's linen. Since Mr. Davies was lingering over Cassandra's hand and Lord Devenham continued to gaze fatuously at his beloved, only the ladies were free to watch the servant's approach. Cassandra, finding the valet's look of amusement at the prolonged hand kiss the outside of enough, pointedly shifted her gaze just in time to see Mrs. Alden's disinterested glance at Godfrey change first to incredulity and then to shock.

The valet also shifted his attention from the hand-kissing

tableau in time to catch the widow's strange reaction. Then he evaporated so quickly through Lord Severn's door that later Cassandra wondered if she had merely imagined the warning look directed at Mrs. Alden and accompanied by a slight shake of the valet's head. Certainly Mrs. Alden's face gave no further clue to the incident, if incident there had been. For she was now exclaiming over the appointments of her chamber as Lord Devenham, followed by his daughter and Mr. Davies, ushered her inside. Cassandra was forced to conclude that in her overwrought state she had suffered a severe delusion. No telling look could possibly have passed between her father's fiancée and her cousin's valet. The notion was absurd.

"My word, that was close!" Charles closed the door behind him and leaned against it weakly. It should have given him a clue concerning his best friend's state of mind that George did not respond to this announcement. Nor did the viscount launch a protest when his valet chose to mop a perspiring brow with the starched cravat atop the pile of linen. "Do you know who I ran into out in the hall, George?" The question, fortunately, was rhetorical. "Gwenny Alden, that's who. And, my God, for a minute there I thought she was going to let the cat right out of the bag. I mean to say, her eyes actually bugged and her jaw dropped at the sight of me. I tell you, it wouldn't have surprised me one bit if she'd blurted out, 'Charles Danforth, whatever are you doing here?' I barely managed to tip her a nod just in time to stop her. But I would have thought Gwenny was too fly by half to get into such a taking."

"What you really thought," George said dully, "was that no one would look at you." George had changed his room and his chair, but his posture and demeanor had not varied since the library episode. He still looked like a man impaled. "Told you that was nonsense."

"Well, you were right, old man." Charles placed the linen on a shell-shaped couch and absently sat down upon it. "I'm going to have to be more careful from now on.

Gwenny will be all right, I'm sure, once I get a chance to have a private word with her. She's a real sport and won't give me away. But do you know who she's brought with her?'' This time the captain waited for an answer. But when none was immediately forthcoming, he filled the void. ''Plumb Davies!''

''Plumb Davies?'' He had succeeded at last in capturing his friend's attention. ''Plumb Davies,'' George repeated. ''Plumb down here with Gwenny?'' A gleam of hope was seen to flicker in the viscount's hitherto dull eyes. ''Were there any other coves?''

''None that I saw. But Plumb's enough. Known me for donkey's years. And what's more, I know for a fact he's staked a bundle on his horse to win the steeplechase. And he's in debt right up to his eyebrows. Lord, he'd love to nobble me if he got a chance.''

''Dammit, Charles!'' Anger had replaced the viscount's despair. He sat bolt upright. ''Can't you get your mind off your own curst affairs for one curst minute? Tell me what you think Plumb's chances are.''

''With me riding Trafalgar? Nil to none, I'd say. Where's your loyalty, old man? Not planning to cover your bets, are you?''

''Not his chances in the steeplechase, you numbskull! His chances with Cassandra! That's what he's here for.''

''Plumb Davies and Cassandra? You must be out of your mind, George.''

''I'm that, all right.'' His tone was bitter. ''But not in the way you mean. Plumb's here for Cassie right enough. Gwenny and Uncle Devenham worked it out together. He gave me to understand that she was going to bring along a whole gaggle of suitors, though. You're sure she didn't?''

''Plumb was all I saw.''

Lord Severn groaned. ''Well, tell me honestly, Charlie. Don't try to spare me. Do you think he stands a chance of pulling the thing off?''

Charles considered the matter thoughtfully. ''Well, he's years older than Lady Cassandra, of course.''

''That's so.'' George groaned again.

"But then some women prefer older men. Gives 'em a better run at widowhood. Why, look at Gwenny."

George brightened. "And he does have a reputation as a ladies' man."

Charles chuckled wickedly. "And have you noticed how he only falls in love when his pockets are to let? He was practically betrothed to Iris Randall two years ago. Then he won a packet playing faro and the romance cooled in no time."

George was glum once again. "That's true. And the thing is, Cassie ain't actually all that wealthy. Not to compare to Lady Iris. So I'm not sure Plumb will make that big a push. Depends, I expect, on how far up the River Tick he is."

Charles was looking at his friend with some astonishment. "I say, George, surely you can't be hoping that Plumb Davies will marry your cousin Cassandra?"

"You're deuced right I am."

Charles was shocked. "But, George, the man's a here-and-thereian. Got no background. Went to Eton on a king's scholarship! Lives by his wits. Can't fault him for that, I suppose. Actually, he's a damned shrewd gamester, but a gamester all the same. Not at all the sort of cove one wishes to see married to one's cousin."

"Not under normal circumstances, maybe. But any old port in a storm, they say. You've heard the expression, Charles?"

"Of course I've heard it. But what does it have to say to anything?"

"Just that if it's a choice between Cassandra marrying Plumb Davies or Cassandra marrying me, well, there's no getting away from it, my preference is for Plumb."

"That's not exactly a noble sentiment, George, old man, but I suppose it's understandable. What isn't, though, is why you'd give Lady Cassandra such a Hobson's choice. It's my opinion that she ain't likely to want to marry either one of you. Or, when it comes to that, she don't seem exactly eager to marry at all. Her heart's set on raising horses."

"I know all that." George ran his fingers through his hair, a thing he'd never have done under normal circumstances. The disarrangement, however, was hardly noticeable, so far had his Titus already strayed from its classic lines. "But it don't make a tuppence worth of difference what Cassandra wants. It's what her old Roman of a father wants that counts. And he's dead set on her marrying somebody. And"—he groaned pathetically while clutching handfuls of the abused hair—"he thinks I've offered for her."

Charles was becoming gravely concerned about his friend. He did realize that the absence of Chesney had put a considerable strain on George's fastidious nature, but he hadn't expected it to unhinge him altogether. "Oh, come now, George, that's absurd. Why on earth would Lord Devenham think a thing like that?"

"Damned if I know. Thought I was making myself perfectly clear. But the fact is, the old horror wasn't half listening. Never seems to when I talk, even in the ordinary way of things. And this time his mind was set on Gwenny. Kept jumping up to race to the window to look out and see if she was coming. No wonder he put me off my stride. I'd rehearsed the whole thing a hundred times. For under the best of circumstances it's devilish tricky asking a man to let his unmarried daughter set up on her own. And with him up and down all the time like a jumping jack, no wonder I made a mull of it. Then when the old widgeon finally did listen, all my talk about Cassie's future gave him the wrong idea. He thought I was offering for her."

There was a moment of silence. Conflicting emotional responses warred on Captain Danforth's face. Just as one seemed about to gain ascendency, the viscount headed it off.

"I'm warning you right now, Charlie, if you laugh—no, not even that—if you don't wipe that smirk off your face this instant, your masquerade is finished. I'll march straight out of this room to find Plumb Davies and tell him that you're here. Then it's up to him to get in touch with Bow Street. I'll be sending for Chesney."

"You wouldn't do that and you know it, George. Far too good a friend. Besides, I ain't going to laugh. But really, old fellow, aren't you making a bit too much of this? All you have to do is tell his lordship he mistook your meaning."

"That's all? All?" The viscount's voice had a hollow ring to it. "Have you seen my uncle in a temper? He'll be sure to think that I'm only trying to weasel out of the thing. If he don't get out the horsewhip, I'll be amazed."

"Well, then, let Lady Cassandra tell him."

"You think I ain't already thought of that?" The viscount gave his friend a withering look. "The thing is, she don't want to."

"My word, don't tell me she's going to hold you to it? Wouldn't've thought she was the sort to take advantage of a man trying to do her a favor."

"No, it ain't like that. She don't want to marry me any more than I do her. Thing is, she don't want any part of Gwenny's matchmaking. She reasons that as long as her father thinks she's betrothed to me he won't be throwing Davies—or any other candidate—at her head."

"Well, now, that does make sense."

"Of course it does. But it also leaves me holding the bag."

"That's not exactly a gallant way of putting it, but I do see what you mean, George. Just how long is this little charade to go on?"

"It's Cassandra's idea that we should just go along with things till after her papa's wedding. She says Uncle Devenham's unlikely to spare us a thought, anyhow. Then when he's back from his wedding trip, she'll break the news that it's all a big misunderstanding."

"Well, that sounds reasonable enough. Certainly should make your stay here more pleasant."

" 'Reasonable?' I tell you, Charlie, you don't use the word *reasonable* and Uncle Devenham in the same breath. The more I think on it, the more I think Cassie's head is full of maggots. You just don't know how desperate Uncle is to get her married off. It's all very well to say he's so smitten that he won't think of anything else but Gwenny. But how long does it take to send a notice to the *Gazette*?"

"You think he'll do that?"

"In a flash. The only thing holding him back right now is that he's had Gwenny out beating the bushes for other beaux and he don't want her to think she's wasted her time. But, oh, lord, if all she's come up with is Plumb Davies . . . Well, even Uncle Devenham will think I'm better husband material than Plumb."

"I'm afraid you're right there, George."

"But then, of course"—the reluctant fiancé brightened up a bit—"if Cassandra were actually to fall in love with Plumb, well, I don't think Uncle would throw a rub in her way. He ain't all that fond of me."

"Do you think that's apt to happen?" The captain sounded doubtful.

But George had become a drowning man overestimating the buoyancy of his straw. "Well, you never can tell with females, can you? They tend to fall in love with all sorts of peculiar coves. The more unsuitable the better."

"That's very true." The captain's hearty tone somehow lacked the ring of true conviction. "But just in case, George, would it really be so bad? Marrying Lady Cassandra, I mean. You will have to marry someday. And she strikes me as a rather good sort. A trifle overbearing, perhaps. But have you seen her on a horse?"

The viscount glared. "When I do get married, Charlie, I'd like it to be from choice, not necessity. And when I choose a bride, it won't be on the basis of how she sits a horse."

"Well, suit yourself. Seems as good a way as any. But in the meantime, what are you going to do?"

"I don't know." His lordship sank back in his chair once more, in an attitude of total despair. His friend watched him sympathetically for a while, then removed himself from the pile of linen and transferred it to a bow-fronted chest of drawers.

"Eureka!" The viscount's shout caused Charles to slam the drawer on his finger. "We'll sneak out of here. That's what. We'll do what the Runner chap advised you to do. Go to France. Leave tonight. My treat, Charlie.''

Charles Danforth bent a look of sorrow on his friend as he sucked his injured digit. "I can't do that, George. Remember? The race. I've got to ride in the race. It's the only way to pay that debt off. If you go to France, I stay. But that's all right, George.'' There was perhaps a touch of Machiavelli in the captain's look and tone of martyred resignation. "You needn't worry about me. I'll find somewhere else to hide. There's bound to be an empty shed around here somewhere. And I should be able to steal enough from the gardens to stay alive. Of course there is the matter of Trafalgar . . .''

"Oh, damn you, Charlie.''

"Just as you say, George.''

"All right, then. I'll stick it out for your sake. But in the meantime, by God, there are two things you can do for me.''

"Anything, George, old thing. Just name it,'' the captain replied.

"Well, first, you've got to do everything in your power to make sure Plumb Davies wins Cassandra's hand.''

"Now just how the devil do you think I— Oh, well, yes. Indeed. Certainly. Anything you say, George. Now what's the second thing?''

"I want you to break an arm, Charlie. Now. Immediately.''

Chapter Seven

A sling can be a decided handicap to a man perched two stories high on a narrow ledge, hugging the stone wall of a house. Charles Danforth slipped his left arm out of the black silk scarf and inched back a little closer to the open window. In his precipitous haste to leave Gwendolen Alden's room, he had scrambled along the stone tightrope a bit too far. Now he needed to be within earshot to determine when the coast was clear.

Charles was thankful for the darkness as he played at being a human fly. He didn't want to think, let alone see, just how far the distance was to the ground. It was a bit past midnight. Not only had Gwenny been tediously tardy about returning to her room, where he'd been waiting for a private word with her, but he'd barely begun to explain why he was posing as a valet and was nowhere near asking for discretion on her part when the door to her bedchamber had creaked. The silly wench had failed to latch it! The warning had given Charles just enough time to scramble out the open window before a nightshirted Lord Devenham had come creeping into the boudoir of his betrothed.

Now, as the captain inched closer, the sounds emerging from the bedchamber were enough to put a less worldly fellow to the blush. Charles inclination was to curse. He nipped it in the bud and thought instead.

Obviously, Lord Devenham's visit was to be of some duration. Indeed, he was probably situated for the night. And there was a limit to just how long a cove could go on clinging to a wall. Suppressing a sigh, Charles crept away.

He thanked his lucky stars and Providence for the English addiction to fresh air. The next window in line was open. He paused to listen. All was quiet inside. He risked a peek. No candle burned. It did seem safe to enter.

Sleep had eluded Cassandra Devenham. In earlier, more tranquil times, the only prerequisite was for her head to touch the pillow. Now the turmoil of her life required other measures. But her sheep-counting had been interrupted moments before by faint, scrambling sounds coming from outside her window. She had listened intently. Then they had come again. Abandoning the notion of an outsized squirrel afflicted with insomnia, she had crept from her bed to investigate. Now she stood, water pitcher poised, as Charles Danforth eased his way across her sill.

Some inborn instinct, honed perhaps at Waterloo, caused the cavalry captain to pitch forward in the nick of time. The pitcher swooshed in a harmless arc above his head. But the contents cascaded down upon him. "Bloody hell!" Charles Danforth sputtered. "What did you do that for? I'll catch my death."

"Nonsense! Is that you, Godfrey?"

Cassandra was in the act of exchanging her pitcher for a poker, which she then proceeded to press down upon the intruder's shoulder as if dubbing him a knight. "Explain yourself—if you think you can," she commanded in a whisper.

"Well. . . ." She had planted the seed of doubt in Charles's mind. "It won't be easy," he whispered back. "And it really would help if you wouldn't press that poker quite so hard. Not Spartan to mention it, but there is the matter of my broken arm.''

''Your what?''

''Broken arm. Normally doesn't bother me all that much, but a pressing poker ain't really quite the thing.''

Cassandra was in a quandary. Naturally kindhearted, she didn't care to cause a fellow creature pain. But on the other hand she didn't trust the slippery valet above half. She opted for a bluff. ''Very well, then. I shall remove the poker. But just bear in mind, Godfrey, I have my pistol trained on you.''

''Very well, m'lady,'' Charles replied meekly, slipping his arm back into the sling as he scrambled to his feet. ''Mind if I sit down a bit?'' He groped his way toward a massive silhouette.

''Not on the bed!''

''Whyever not?''

''Well, for one thing, you're wet.''

''That's hardly my fault. But whatever you say, miss. I could just faint right here on the floor.'' Uttering a piteous moan, he collapsed thereupon with a dull thud.

''Bloody hell!'' Lady Cassandra exclaimed for the first and final time in her entire life.

She scrambled over his prone body to reach the bedside candle and strike a light, then held the taper aloft with a shaky hand. Its pale glow was reflected back by the white teeth of the grinning valet. ''Got you, m'lady!''

''That's not funny, Godfrey! Nor will you find the situation quite so amusing when I open the door and shout for help.''

''Oh, but I really don't think you should do that, Lady Cassandra.''

''Whyever not? I've caught you red-handed, sneaking into my room. Of course I intend to have you taken into custody.''

''Well, it's not for the likes of me, of course, to tell the gentry what to do.'' He held his arm pathetically while rising. ''But I must point out one thing. It won't look good.''

"That goes without saying, Godfrey. Robbery does carry with it a certain unsavory connotation."

"Robbery!" His voice rose with horror. He quickly lowered it. "You surely can't be thinking I climbed in here to rob you! And with one arm at that! I tell you, miss, I ain't that enterprising."

Cassandra was momentarily diverted. "How on earth did you break your arm?"

"Fell off my horse."

She sniffed disdainfully. "Well, it seems I've overestimated your equestrian skill as well as your honesty. I must say, you're an all-around disappointment, Godfrey."

"Yes, I can see as how I might be. And I'm that sorry for it. But now, if you could just allow me to sneak out of here—for it's obvious that due to your quick action I haven't lifted anything—well, then, we won't have to set any suspicious types that may have noticed us out riding together to wondering if I really came in here to nab your jewelry or for a different reason."

For the first time Cassandra became mindful of the dishabille that Charles had been conscious of all along. Though he'd found her undiaphanous nightdress a disappointment, he had to admit that her ladyship did look quite fetching with her vulnerable bare feet and her nightcap all askew on tousled curls.

The object of his stare was coloring. "No one saw us out riding together this morning. Besides, only a lewd sort of imagination would jump to the kind of conclusion you imply."

"Oh, I couldn't agree more, m'lady. Only, begging your pardon, you'd be amazed at just how many imaginations of that sort there are around."

Cassandra was thinking furiously. She voiced her thought in a grudging whisper. "Oh, very well, then. I don't see that it would serve any purpose to rouse the household. As you pointed out, you haven't had the chance to steal anything. And it's safe to assume that you won't rob anyone else now that I'm on to you. For I tell you right now, Godfrey, if one of my guests misses as much as a snuffbox, it's gaol for you, my man. But as things stand now, I merely intend to report you to my cousin in the morning and see to it that you're packed off back to London. Now go—before I change my mind and have you tied up in the cellars." Cassandra gestured dramatically toward the door.

"Thank you, m'lady," Charles murmured meekly as he bowed. He tiptoed to the door, cautiously opened it a crack, then closed it quickly and leaned against it.

"Go, I said!" Cassandra hissed.

"I can't. There's a footman sitting in the hall staring this way."

"Oh, my heavens, I forgot! Lord Morice!"

"I beg your pardon?"

"Lord Morice. He has the room across the hall, and he's notorious about his candles. Puts 'em out by sticking them under his pillow. Or else he simply throws them across the floor. We always station a servant by his door to watch for fires while he's in the house."

"Very prudent, I'm sure. How long will he be out there?"

"Who knows? You'll just have to go out the way you came."

Charles paled a bit. "I don't think I can do that again, your ladyship. In fact, if I'd had time to think before, I wouldn't have done it in the first place."

"Oh, for goodness sake! You're a fine one to take up a life of crime. Don't tell me you're like a kitten in a tree. You can go up a ladder but not down again."

"What ladder's that, miss?"

"Why, the one you came up on."

"I'm afraid there isn't any ladder."

"Don't be ridiculous." Cassandra carried the candle over to the window to prove her point. She held it high as she leaned out perilously. Her eyes were wide when she turned back to face the valet, who had followed her. "How ever did you manage to get in here?"

Charles felt a wave of giddiness as he recalled the narrowness of the ledge he'd perched upon. "It don't even bear thinking on, m'lady."

All the same, Cassandra did think on it. She reached the candle into the outer darkness once again and gazed down upon the narrow toehold that decoratively divided the house's stories. Her bedchamber was on the corner—and next to it . . . ! She turned accusingly toward the intruder. "You came from Mrs. Alden's room!" she hissed.

The valet neither denied nor confirmed this accusation, unless a slight heightening of color counted as an admission. "And what's more," her ladyship continued, "I'll bet a monkey you did not go in there with robbery in mind."

"Told you I wasn't any thief."

"As for what you are, Godfrey, well, I'm too much of a lady to put a name to that."

"See now. Even you are doing it," Charles said.

"Doing what?"

"Jumping to evil-minded conclusions. Just like you said no one was likely to do if they saw me coming out of *your* room."

"I assure you, Godfrey, these two situations are not at all the same. I happened to note Mrs. Alden's reaction when she saw you this morning. She nearly jumped right out of her skin."

"Oh, that. Well, now, I expect that I probably reminded her of someone else. I do look like a lot of other coves."

Cassandra snorted. "Fustian! You don't look like anybody else I ever saw."

"But then your ladyship ain't as widely acquainted as Mrs. Alden."

The conversation seemed to have strayed away from the main issue. Cassandra firmly jerked it back. "I want you out of my bedchamber, Godfrey. You can go back the way you came."

"I'm afraid I can't do that, m'lady."

"Afraid?" she sneered. "If you managed before, you can do so again."

"Well, laying aside the issue of my courage and even supposing I don't plunge to my death—"

"The fall likely won't kill you."

"And what's a few more broken bones? You're hard, m'lady," Charles complained. "But have you stopped to think that even if I manage to make it back to Mrs. Alden's chamber, your fire-preventing footman has almost as good a view of her door as he has of yours?"

"Well, at least there'd be some justice in her loss of reputation."

"That's unworthy of your ladyship, if I may say so."

Cassandra did feel rather ashamed of the remark but refused to show it. "Well, since you're so concerned for Mrs. Alden's character, you can lurk in *her* bedchamber till the footman goes to sleep or leaves. The thing is, I want you out of mine. Now go!" The same dramatic gesture she'd used formerly for the door was now directed toward the window.

The valet sighed. "Much as I'd like to oblige your ladyship, I can't do that." He stopped her rebuttal by holding up a restraining hand. "You surely can't be thinking I became a human fly by choice. The fact is, m'lady, Mrs. Alden ain't alone."

"You mean . . . ?"

The valet nodded. And in the stunned silence that followed, the unmistakable sounds of a bed creaking came drifting on the breeze that crossed the windowsill.

"Before the wedding has taken place! But that's—that's shocking!"

"Oh, I wouldn't go so far as all that, m'lady. So what if human nature got a bit of a jump on the clergyman? It's the intent that counts, I'd say."

For that bit of philosophy, he earned a withering look. "Well, what's to be done now?" Cassandra muttered to herself.

"If I could make a suggestion, m'lady."

"Yes?"

"You could climb back into bed and get your rest. I'll just stretch out here on this sofa"—Charles looked dubiously at an uncomfortable-appearing piece of furniture adorned with gilt lions' heads—"checking every so often on your footman to see if the coast is clear. Then when you wake up in the morning, I'll be gone.''

"I'll do no such thing!"

"Well, then, do you mind if I just sit on the sofa while you stand over me with the poker?'' he asked. "It's been a long and trying evening—and there is the matter of my arm.''

"Oh, very well. Sit then.'' Cassandra tiptoed to the door and eased it open. The conscientious servant maintained his post with folded arms and wide-open eyes. She closed the door. "Oh, botheration!"

She crossed the room to perch primly on a chair opposite the valet, placing the candle on the table between them. The dignified silence she'd intended to maintain was marred by an increased volume of the amorous sounds coming from next door. To cover them, she asked, "How well do you know Mrs. Alden?'' Immediately, she longed to retract the question.

It wasn't necessary. "You don't like the lady much, now, do you?'' he said evasively.

"I don't *know* the lady much. But, no, I don't expect we shall deal well together.''

"You could be pleasantly surprised. She's a good-enough sort. Or so I'm told.'' Here was a golden opportunity to do his best friend a service. "You must admit, m'lady, it was good of Mrs. Alden to bring Mr. Davies here to meet you.''

"I'll admit nothing of the kind. Mr. Davies is here as Mrs. Alden's friend. It has nothing to do with me.''

"If you say so, miss.''

"And why should I be grateful to have an old roué flung at my head?'' she asked.

"He ain't so old. Quite a bit shy of fifty, I'd say. As for that other word, I'm not sure what you mean.''

"Old rake, then.''

"Well, I suppose that part's true enough. But then I thought ladies tended to like a man who knows his way around.''

"You would think so. But putting the rest aside, I think Mr. Davies's interest is fixed on Mrs. Alden."

"Plumb and Gwenny? Meaning no disrespect, I intended to say Mr. Davies and Mrs. Alden," Charles added hastily. "Well, they are close friends. Always have been. But that's all. Look, miss, if I may so so, I think you're being too hard on Mrs. Alden. Your papa could do worse. I think she'll make him a capital wife. And while we're letting our hair down, I don't think you should be so prejudiced against every man you meet. Why, Mr. Davies may turn out to be a prince of a fellow. At least old Plumb's ripe for the picking, anyhow." He chuckled at the pun.

"Actually, you're merely trying to get your master off the hook, now, aren't you?" When the valet looked guilty at the shrewd question, Cassandra continued. "Just why George chose to confide in you passes all understanding, but you—or he—needn't worry. I've no intention of trapping George into marriage."

"He knows that, m'lady. Still, you must admit it would solve a lot of problems if you could see your way clear to accepting Mr. Davies. I think your father would be pleased."

"Well, if Papa prefers Mr. Davies to George, he's more addlepated than I've suspected. And as for pleasing him, heaven knows I'd like to. Nothing more. But I've never done so in my life and I'm not likely to begin now."

The valet grimaced. "That way, is it? Well, I can sympathize. I've never succeeded in pleasing my father, either."

"With me it began at birth. I was the wrong sex, you see," Cassandra explained.

"My sex wasn't a problem. The order of my birth was. Second son, you see. My brother was a regular paragon. Could do no wrong."

"And you were jealous?"

"No, believe it or not, I wasn't. Relieved would be more accurate. For since I couldn't hope to touch him in perfection, it opened up several more interesting avenues for me." Charles chuckled wickedly. "The problem only came when Winfield died and Papa expected me to become just like him. That sort of metamorphosis was impossible, of course.''

"As impossible as me becoming male.''

"Oh, worse. I've seen you ride.'' He grinned.

"Oh, I say, Godfrey, was Winfield a butler?''

He looked startled. "What makes you ask? I mean, however did you conclude that?''

"Well, it's the only logical explanation.'' Her eyes sparkled with the challenge of detection. "I mean, it's the only reasonable explanation of why you're so misplaced in life. And aspiring to be a butler, of all things. That has to be it. You're trying to be like your brother to please your father.''

"By George!'' He looked at her admiringly.

"Don't do it, Godfrey.''

"I beg your pardon?''

"It doesn't work. Trying to be something that you're not. You have to be true to yourself, no matter what.''

"Yes, m'lady.''

"You can't make yourself responsible for anyone else's unhappiness. You'll only wind up making two people miserable. You shouldn't try to be a house servant. You should work with horses.''

"You'll hire me, then, when you get your establishment?''

Awash with missionary zeal, Cassandra was just about to acquiesce when an internal warning bell began to peal. Employ Godfrey? It didn't bear contemplating! "Well, I can't commit myself to that,'' she hedged. "But I tell you what I will do,'' she added in a burst of inspiration. "If I ever get my own stables, that is. I'll hire Trafalgar for stud and pay you handsomely.''

"Well,'' the valet said with a sigh, "I'm glad you think that at least one of us has possibilities. Too bad it had to be the horse. If you do get your own establishment, I'll consider it. But the more I think on it, I doubt that will ever happen. It's my opinion that Mr. Davies, or someone else, will see past the starchiness and the old-maidish hairstyle and clothes and discover the real woman I'm looking at right now. And you'll be at the altar before you can say 'Jack Robinson,' and will forget all about Trafalgar and myself.''

An unsettling gleam in the valet's eyes jarred Cassandra back to the realities of her situation. Lady Cassandra Devenham, in her nightgown, tête-à-tête with a womanizing servant in her bedroom in the wee hours of the night! She shuddered at the scandal that would ensue if the situation became known. No one would believe that their little chat had had all the propriety of a drawing-room morning call. If one received servants in a drawing room, that is. Her cheeks burned with shame. Why did this particular member of the lower class keep throwing her off balance? As if her life wasn't topsy-turvy enough without his impudent intrusion!

The valet seemed to be reading her thoughts. ''Perhaps I'd better check again to see whether the coast is clear.''

''No, let me look. Jules might see you peeping out.'' She eased the door open a tiny crack while Charles stood behind it. The footman's chair was empty. ''It's all right.'' She turned to reassure the valet. ''You can go now,'' she whispered.

Afterward, while blowing a cloud in the viscount's dressing room, Charles concluded that his action at that point had been purely reflexive. Good manners had also played a part. How else did one leave a lady's boudoir after a midnight rendezvous? But for whatever reason, taking no time for thought, at the point of departure he had found himself pulling Lady Cassandra into his arms, pressing the soft curves of her body, all too evident under the loose-fitting cotton nightdress, against his own in a fashion designed to set his heart to thudding and to send the blood rushing into his ears. And not content with merely that much havoc, he had brought his mouth down hungrily upon hers.

But safely ensconced on his cot at last, lying listening to the viscount snore next door, away from the pliant body and the sweet, tender lips of the lady, Charles cursed himself for an impulsive fool. Wasn't his life in enough disarray without adding more complications?

Charles Danforth's turmoil was not, however, a remarkable circumstance compared to the state Cassandra Devenham was left in. For her, the kiss had been total devastation. She was far too honest to pretend that she had not thrilled to the feel of Godfrey's lips upon her own. And, oh, dear heavens, had she actually kissed a valet back? Her cheeks burned with humiliation and something else less recognizable. It wasn't fair! It was too lowering! That a valet—the very term brought on a shudder—should cause her to feel this way! It didn't bear thinking of. She *wouldn't* think of it any longer. And tomorrow she'd have George send the impudent fellow packing.

Cassandra tossed and turned and fumed, and finally toward morning had almost drifted off to sleep when a new thought struck her. She sat bolt upright. "That scoundrel used both arms!" she said aloud.

Chapter Eight

*T*he Viscount Severn *rotated slowly before the cheval* glass. He not only rotated; the fact was, he preened. For George knew perfection when he saw it. His pomaded locks, coaxed and curled into place, out-Titused Titus. The high points of his snowy collar were so stiff they stood in danger of slicing off his ears. No speck of lint marred the perfection of his bottle-green coat. His biscuit-colored pantaloons hugged his thighs and were free of spots and wrinkles. His Hessians gleamed with blacking and champagne. Another orbit brought George full-face once more before the looking glass. His sigh was one of pure contentment. Behind him, the valet frowned.

"I'm sorry, sir. The cravat. It's not quite right. I do beg pardon. If we could try again . . . ?"

"It isn't?" George peered into the glass. By gad, the chap was right. To think he'd missed a detail like that. Just went to show how far his standards had slipped in the past few days. He obediently sat back down at the dressing table and watched with satisfaction while the valet un-wound the offending neckcloth and prepared to try again.

Lord Severn's spirits were on the rise. It was not in his nature to stay in the slough of despondency too long. This morning, when the sun was shining and the gloom of night was a phantom of the past, it was easy to believe that his cousin Cassandra would not allow herself—and him—to be bullied to the altar. And he could not help but congratulate himself on the stroke of genius that had extricated him from an even worse fate—having Charles Danforth as his valet.

Getting Charlie to fake a broken arm was brilliant, even if he did say so himself. And then, in his valetless state, what could have been more natural than to appeal to Plumb Davies for help? Next to his own Chesney, Davies's man was top of the trees. And since Plumb's pockets were to let, George knew he'd take the hint and offer to share the services of his valet. For a fee, of course.

There was one thing, however. George frowned at the glass. (Misinterpreting the look, Standen the valet mur-mured, "Just so, sir," and ever so slightly adjusted one end of the viscount's neckcloth.) The figure Plumb had mentioned seemed excessive. Exorbitant, in fact. Plumb had admitted as much himself. "I realize you're desperate, old man. Still, I don't want you to think I'm taking advan-tage of your sartorial crisis. You see, along with Standen's services, I'm throwing in a bonus. I'm wearing blinders. Can't see a thing that I don't look straight at."

Dash the fellow, anyhow. George did hate coves who had to be so cryptic. But when he'd told Plumb that he hadn't the vaguest notion what he was talking about, the older man had laughed and said in that case, well, he didn't either, but if George didn't mind, they'd keep the price of Standen's services up there all the same. "Just in case my memory comes back." He'd emphasized again that he hated to take advantage of another man's misfortune, but the fact was, he needed to up his wagering for the cross-country race. "Now that your friend Danforth's in France"—he'd winked—"my horse is the favorite, you know. You should put a bit on Thunderer yourself, George."

That conclusion to the conversation had effectively squelched George's original suspicion that Davies had somehow tumbled to the fact that Charles was on the premises. Charles, too, was sure that Plumb hadn't seen him. "Gwenny might have told him I'm here, though," he'd added thoughtfully. "I'll ask her the first chance I get."

The viscount shook off his worries and gave one long, last, satisfied stare at his reflection. Well, even if Davies did know about Charles, he'd been paid to hold his tongue. And no price was too high in order to look like a gentleman once more. George thanked Standen with choked sincerity and went down to breakfast.

The viscount's spirits weren't the only ones on the rise. Plumb Davies was feeling more in tune with the world than he had for ages. Only desperation could have made him give in to Gwenny and accompany her to Hampshire. Rustication was not his cup of tea. Nor was he eager to pursue Devenham's spinster daughter.

But the streak of luck that had lined his pockets by way of his valet's talent seemed fated to continue. Lady Cassandra improved on acquaintance. Sans the fragrance of horse, she showed possibilities. True, her taste in clothes was deplorable, but he could remedy that. With a little attention to style, she could be quite attractive. Of course having old prosy Devenham for a papa-in-law hardly bore thinking of. Still, he chuckled aloud, that would be more than compensated for, by having Gwenny for a mama-in-law. Pity, though, that the girl's fortune wasn't larger. Still, he could always count on Gwenny to come up with the ready when he needed it.

That evening, not being one to allow the grass to grow beneath his feet, Mr. Davies contrived to take Lady Cassandra in to dinner, where he pressed his advantage further by asking her to show him the rose garden after the repast. He saw her hesitate and could have sworn she was about to fob him off until her cousin, who had been watching them intently throughout the meal at the expense of his own dinner partner, gave her a glare that prompted her to accept the invitation politely, if without enthusiasm.

When they took the air three-quarters of an hour later, Cassandra soon realized that Mr. Davies was not half as interested in roses as he'd claimed to be. In fact, as they strolled along the stone pathway that wove through the various plantings like enormous ribbons tied around giant nosegays, he seemed rather amused by her horticulture lecture. It was the London Season all over again, Cassandra thought with the chagrin that recollection always cost her. Her father was right. She hadn't the slightest notion of how to talk to gentlemen. "I'm boring you, am I not?" she blurted out.

"Quite the contrary, Lady Cassandra," he avowed solemnly. But even in the fading daylight she could see the twinkle in his eyes. He was actually rather handsome, she supposed, in an elderly, foppish sort of way. She should, she knew, be enjoying his attention.

"I have never been so well instructed by a lady's conversation," he continued. "Indeed, I'd no idea there was so much information to be gained about roses. I fear I've always taken them too much for granted. But no longer will I wear a wine-red boutonniere or present a pale pink blossom to a lady without thinking of the miracles that enabled those roses to survive despite inclimate weather and the myriad pests bent on their destruction. And just what sort of fertilizer did you say your gardeners use? Sheep manure was certainly mentioned, I recall."

"Now you are laughing at me, Mr. Davies."

"I would never do that, dear lady. But I do admit that I find you far more fascinating—and need I say it, more lovely—than your garden." On the pretext of helping her cross a small wooden bridge that arched over a brook, which was gurgling and swollen from a recent rain, he caught her hand in his. The scent of flowers hung heavily on the humid air. The trees and bushes were newly washed a vivid green. The setting seemed to be waiting for romance. Cassandra wished she'd stayed inside.

After guiding her safely across the perils of the wooden structure, Mr. Davies did not see fit to let go of her hand. "Careful of the stones, m'dear. They can be quite slippery."

"That's true. Perhaps we should go back indoors. I should hate to fall."

His chuckles was soft and intimate. "Oh, I don't think you've anything to fear, sweet lady. I'm the one imperiled. And I don't mean from the paving stones. I fear my downfall from another source."

Fustian! Cassandra barely managed not to say the word aloud. She did wish that this aging beau would not practice his flummery on her. Now he was leading her toward a rustic bench, which was backed by a tall and dripping hedge.

"Could we not sit down a moment and further our acquaintance?"

"It's too wet." Cassandra's tone was at least as dampening as the bench might prove to be.

"Well, yes, perhaps you're right. A pity. Still, though, it's possible to become acquainted on our feet."

Oh, botheration! Cassandra thought as she was crushed in an embrace. This really was the outside of enough!

Her annoyance was mainly directed at herself, however, and not at Mr. Davies. For after the past night's similar occurrence, she should have been alerted for this sort of thing. She was not used to being so slow a learner. But "once bitten, twice shy" seemed not to apply in this particular category.

One thing, however, was very plain. She was not enjoying these caresses. But when she tried to tell Mr. Davies so, his lips grew more insistent and he clasped her tighter still. Cassandra's struggles only seemed to stimulate his passion. Trying to break free proved futile. Though very little taller than herself and slightly built, Mr. Davies showed amazing strength. Recognizing that she could never match it, Cassandra resorted to her wits. She suddenly cooperated. In her ardor she bent her suitor backward. Then, with one satin slipper placed behind his heel, she managed to insinuate her hands against Mr. Davies's chest and give a sudden shove. Her scheme worked beautifully. In part. He did go tumbling backward, landing amidst the roses that lined the path. The problem was, he took Cassandra with him.

"Oof!" Mr. Davies's breath was knocked from his body by the impact. His grip was also loosened, and Cassandra scrambled to her feet. Her first impulse was to sprint off down the path. She repressed it. For one thing, it was too undignified by half, not to mention rather missish. For another, she was no longer concerned about Mr. Davies's passion. Now her concern was for his health. His breath, obviously, had returned in full spate, for he lay there cursing. What he was not doing, however, was getting up. "Are you all right, sir?" she inquired politely.

"Of course I'm not all right." He barely restrained himself from adding "you nincompoop!" "Really, Lady Cassandra, did you have to react quite so violently? Surely you've been kissed before!"

As a matter of fact, she had been. Quite recently, at that. But she was not prepared to discuss the matter with this gentleman. "Here, let me help you up, sir," she offered handsomely. Mr. Davies, after all, was no longer young.

"That won't be necessary," he answered huffily, making preliminary motions toward rising to his feet. "Ouch! Damnation! Ouch!"

"Oh, my heavens, whatever is the matter?" She feared the worst. A broken hip, perhaps. And how would she explain it? It was relief that made her giggle when he exclaimed, "I'm stuck in these damn thorns."

"Ain't funny, I can assure you!" There was a ripping sound as he struggled free and regained his feet.

Mr. Davies looked behind him at the ruin of his knee smalls. The white satin was briar-pricked and streaked with mud. A faint trace of the fertilizer they'd so recently discussed assailed their nostrils. The gentleman swore once again. Fluently.

Lady Cassandra, trying hard to compose her features, solicitously plucked out a remaining thorn. Without any apparent effort on his part, Mr. Davies repressed his gratitude for this assistance. "If your ladyship will excuse me"—he bowed stiffly—"I think I had best retire and change." Not waiting, however, for her permission, he set off swiftly down the path.

Cassandra watched his furious withdrawal until the curving walkway took him out of her sight. Then, disregarding its dampened state, she collapsed upon the wooden bench and indulged in the fit of laughter she'd been suppressing. "Oh, dear," she said as she finally controlled herself, wiping her eyes. And then she sniffed. And sniffed again to confirm her first impression. She smelled smoke! Tobacco smoke! Someone somewhere was blowing a cloud! And quite nearby! She turned and gazed suspiciously at the hedge behind her. Sure enough, a thin blue wisp came drifting through the foliage. She sprang to her feet and strode purposefully around the hedge.

"Godfrey!"

The valet was lounging on a bench, the twin of the one Cassandra had just abandoned. It also backed against the hedge. He was puffing thoughtfully on a huge cigar. At the sound of her voice, he adjusted the sling he wore and came respectfully to his feet. The look he bent on her, however, was reproachful. "Your ladyship made a proper mess of things just now, if I may say so."

"Well, you may not!"

"Very well, ma'am."

"And you should be ashamed of yourself. Playing Peeping Tom!"

"Now that's a bit unfair, m'lady. Being situated here as I was before you came along, I couldn't help overhearing, now, could I? But I didn't go peeping through the hedge till I heard a thud and Mr. Davies began to swear. Then I thought that somebody might be needing help. Should have known it wasn't you." His lips twitched suddenly. "Landed him a leveler, did you?"

"Nothing of the sort! I merely gave him a push, that's all."

His face grew grave once more. And then he sighed.

"Now, I realize, m'lady, you only did what you felt you had to, but have you thought of the consequences?"

"Of course I have. My action broke up an encounter of the kind I can only describe as odious."

"Odious, m'lady? Are you speaking only of this specific encounter, or more generally? No, never mind that now. Back to the situation I just overheard—I do feel obliged to point out that you would have done better to accomplish your goal, terminating Mr. Davies's kiss, that is, without totally destroying his dignity in the process. A man doesn't mind appearing a cad half as much as he hates to look the fool."

"No doubt. But just *how*—not even to ask *why*—was I to preserve Mr. Davies's dignity without allowing myself to be ravished? Or is that a matter of no consequence?"

"Oh, come now. Even Pl—er, Mr. Davies would not go that far," Charles protested.

"No? But then you were not as aware as I of how his hands were straying."

"Why, the old lecher!"

"Well, I am pleased to see that you do recognize the type." Lady Cassandra gave the valet a speaking look. He had the grace to appear embarrassed.

"Uh, about last night, your ladyship," he began awkwardly. "I really would like to apologize. I don't quite know what came over me."

"The same thing that came over Mr. Davies, no doubt."

"Well, you do seem to cause us weak creatures of the opposite sex to lose our heads, and that's a fact, m'lady."

"That's nonsense, and you know it, Godfrey. A certain type of man simply feels obliged to act like a barnyard rooster when in the presence of the other sex. You and Mr. Davies just happen to be prime examples of the type. It has little enough to do with me."

The valet rubbed his chin. "Sink me if I know which of the three of us you've most insulted. But right off the reel I'd say it's you, m'lady. You really should stop thinking so little of yourself. Your attitude goes beyond modesty. It's demeaning."

"Don't lecture me, Godfrey!" Lady Cassandra spoke sharply. "Let's discuss you for a change. Will you please explain how it happens you're still at Devenham Hall?"

"I don't quite understand, your ladyship. Lord Severn intends to remain here through the wedding, naturally."

"I know he does. But the only reason I did not ask him to send you packing is that I thought it unnecessary. Since you're no use to him with a broken arm—if, indeed, you ever were of use—I assumed he'd send you back to London without my having to request it. But unless you now arrange your own departure, I see that I will have to speak to my cousin after all."

"But why, m'lady?"

"Why? You surely must see that your overfamiliarity"—her cheeks reddened—"is intolerable. I will not have you at the hall. It's not my character alone I'm concerned with. I fear for Mrs. Alden's reputation as well."

"I think perhaps your ladyship does me too much credit." Charles broke into a sudden grin.

"There's nothing at all amusing in the situation. I shudder to think what would be the outcome if my father should learn of either of your excursions last evening."

The valet shuddered, too. "I do see what you mean, m'lady. But if I was to promise to be the soul of propriety, could I stay? You see, there are some very pressing reasons why Lord Severn needs me here."

"Name one."

"Begging your ladyship's pardon, but I'm not at liberty to say. I can assure your ladyship, however, that you'll never even know I'm on the premises. I'll give my oath on that." Cassandra appeared to waver in her resolve and he pressed his advantage home. "Really, m'lady, if you do ask Lord Severn to ship me back to London, he's bound to want to know the reason why. And while you might not mind telling him, on the other hand you might just find it a bit embarrassing. And as for his lordship—well, he's bound to be upset, and frankly, m'lady, what with his recent, er, betrothal, I don't know how much more strain the poor gentleman can stand. Chances are, he'll funk it and insist on accompanying me back to the metropolis. And leave you unsupported.''

''Hmmm.''

''Besides''—he was gaining ground—''there'll be no repetition of last night, I promise. So what possible harm can my being at Devenham Hall do you?''

Right off, Cassandra could think of several answers to that question, none of which she cared to share with her cousin's valet. But before she could come up with something acceptable, they heard the chatter of approaching strollers. Other guests had decided to take the evening air.

''I'd best be going, m'lady.'' The valet bowed. ''And thank you for giving me a second chance.'' He scrambled through the hedge just before the houseguests could turn the corner. ''You won't be sorry, m'lady.'' The whisper floated through the foliage.

It was just as well that Cassandra was now under observation and unable to reply. For every bit of reason she possessed cried out that, in all likelihood, she was going to be very, very sorry, indeed, not to have seen the last of Godfrey.

Chapter Nine

When Cassandra returned to the drawing room un-accompanied, Mrs. Alden was afire with curiosity. She burned to know what had become of Mr. Davies. She had been longing to make her escape for ages. The evening had turned musical. She had endured three self-accompanied vocal renditions by a distant Devenham relation whose inability to stay on key was matched by a complete lack of talent for the pianoforte. And now another young lady with an overpowering mama was earnestly torturing the harp strings. Really! Was there no end in sight?

Mrs. Alden glanced at Lord Devenham, who was seated in the gilt chair next to her own. He'd been nodding now for ages. Even his starcher could not hold his head erect. His eyes were closed. The time for escape was ripe. Pressing a hand over her mouth as if to stifle a threatening cough, Mrs. Alden fled.

After a fast and futile search of the rose garden, she finally discovered Mr. Davies in his chamber. The gentleman was standing by the window in deference to his host's chairs and his muddy knee smalls while he washed down two hasty glasses of port with a slower third. "Plumb! What on earth?" Mrs. Alden asked as she closed the door behind her.

He turned to face her, his expression bitter. "If you think I'm going to satisfy your morbid curiosity, Gwendolen, you much mistake the matter. Let it suffice to say that I must have been out of my mind to allow you to drag me here. And as for dangling after that—that modern-day Amazon any longer, I'll tell you right now, Mrs. Alden, debtors' prison seems a viable alternative."

Lord Devenham's fiancée put her arms comfortingly around Mr. Davies's neck, at the same time taking care that none of his mud came into contact with her lilac lace. "There, there, now," she gurgled. "Tell me. Has little Cassandra been naughty to Mama's Plumb-boy? And just what did Plumb-boy do to make naughty Cassandra fling mud all over him?"

"This." He bent his head and kissed her, channeling his anger into a more satisfactory sort of passion. When their lips at long last parted, he inquired, "Would any reasonable woman trip a man over a thing like that?"

"Only if she planned to collapse with him," came the husky reply.

"Oh, she did that, all right. Fair flattened me, in fact. But she was on her feet again quick as a cat and just as ready to scratch my eyes out. I tell you, Gwenny, I want no more of that termagant."

"Oh, but you mustn't give up so soon, Plumb-pie," she cooed. "Cassandra's unused to men, that's all. Devenham has kept the poor girl waiting on his comfort hand and foot, and she's had no chance to learn the social graces. Now if only you were a horse"—she giggled and he grinned back—"you'd get along famously.

"But in all seriousness"—she teased his mouth with her index finger—"I don't think I could bear it if you liked the girl too well. I want you to marry her, Plumb, not fall in love with her. Oh, yes, I've quite made up my mind to it. Lady Cassandra is the perfect wife for you.''

His good humor was fast becoming restored. ''Don't be too sure of yourself, Gwenny. The girl's not bad-looking, you may have noticed. Or would be, at any rate, if she knew how to fix herself up a bit. And I could teach her that. What's more, she's still quite young,'' he teased. ''Youth's a definite asset in a woman, don't you know.'' He dodged playfully as Mrs. Alden showed her claws. ''So who's to say I couldn't fall in love with her once I've cured her of her hoyden ways?''

''I'm to say, that's who.'' She buried her face against his shoulder, regardless now of the mud. ''I couldn't bear it.'' Her voice was muffled. ''Any more than I could bear living here if I didn't think I'd have you by my side. You're my only friend, Plumb.''

''Aren't you forgetting Devenham?''

''He'll be my husband. That's not the same.''

''No, thank God.'' He nuzzled his face fondly in her hair, then reluctantly pushed her to arm's length. ''But speaking of Devenham, he'll be wondering what's become of you. And it won't do for him to find you here. He's jealous of me already, in case you haven't noticed.''

''Nonsense. At least no more than he's jealous of any other creature who claims my time.''

''In that case, the more fool he.'' Mr. Davies kissed Mrs. Alden once again, with even less restraint than he'd shown before. ''Go now and let me change.'' He pushed her toward the door. ''Oh, my God!'' He slapped his forehead. ''I almost forgot. To think you'd have that effect, Gwenny, after all these years. Have you talked to Charlie yet?''

''Well''—she dimpled up at him—''he did come to my room last night.''

''The devil he did!'' Mr. Davies frowned. ''So tell me, what besides the obvious did he have on his mind?''

''I couldn't say. There was little time for conversation.''

''Oh, really?'' His eyebrows rose.

''Oh, do take your mind out of bed for a minute, Plumb.

I simply mean that Charlie came sneaking into my room and asked me to pretend I didn't know him. But before I could inquire as to what sort of game he's playing here, Devenham interrupted us.''

"Oh, did he?" He glared. "The path to your bedchamber has become a regular Appian Way. I'll take care not to call."

"Don't worry." She tossed her head. "I can always come to you."

"Knock first. Who knows, I could be entertaining. What's sauce for the goose, as they say. But—forgive my vulgar curiosity—how exactly did you explain Danforth's presence to your possessive fiancé?"

"Thank goodness, I didn't have to. Charlie went out the window."

"Good God! Then he really does have a broken arm."

"Oh, he had that before. But, my heavens! Come to think on it, I haven't seen him since. Could he have broken his neck, Plumb? You did say George Severn has hired your valet."

"Oh, I wouldn't worry about Charlie, my love. I expect he's got more lives than a cat. No, I'm certain he's still around here somewhere. What I need to know is why."

"Well, you told me yourself that the Runners are after him. I think posing as a valet is a capital scheme."

"In a house where any number of people are apt to know him? Don't be goosish. What I find rather more than coincidence is that we're only forty miles from Lower Wallop where the steeplechase is being run. If he's not meaning to ride in it, well, I'm a Frenchman. And his Trafalgar is the only horse around who could possibly beat my Thunderer. So find out what he's up to, Gwenny dear. If he does intend to race Trafalgar, then I may need to change my strategy."

"Well, I can ask. But what makes you think he'll want to tell me?" she asked.

"I don't suppose Samson wanted to tell Delilah what she wished to know, either, but he did so all the same. If you can't worm that bit of information out of the good captain, well, you're not half the woman I take you for.

So go see him tonight, my love, and find out what you can.''

"Oh, very well. If you insist. Delilah to his Samson, eh? Should I take scissors? I may be forced to cut his hair."

"Do as you think best, m'dear. But I hope it doesn't come to that. You mustn't steal my thunder. For some time now, I've longed to be the one to give Captain the Honorable Charles Danforth the trimming he deserves.''

After a midnight supper, the house party had retired, except for those gentlemen engaged in the game of faro that Mr. Davies had proposed and Lord Devenham, with less enthusiasm, had organized; and for those household servants obliged to remain awake to see to the gamesters' refreshment and to prepare them for bed.

Charles Danforth was not happy to be among the group that had settled for the night. Even though he'd taken advantage of George's absence to trade the dressing-room cot for the luxury of the canopied bed, even though he was wearing George's maroon brocade dressing gown, and even though he had helped himself to George's cigars and George's port, he longed to be almost anywhere but where he was.

He would like, for instance, to be playing cards with the gentlemen or to be participating in whatever diversion was to be found in the servants' hall. He'd considered the latter possibility quite seriously, then had reluctantly abandoned it. He was already under too much suspicion there.

Or he'd like to be strolling in the garden with Lady Cassandra. Charles swore under his breath at that unbidden thought and viciously stabbed out the butt of his cigar in the candle holder. That was the trouble with enforced solitude. It gave a cove too dashed much time to think. And it weakened his resistance. Stroll in the garden with Lady Cassandra, indeed. Lord Devenham's daughter represented the very thing he'd been at so much pains to avoid: a period to his freedom.

Charles held his glass toward the candle flame and admired the sparkle of the crystal and the rich color of the wine. The thing was, as he'd tried to explain to his father, he hadn't been bred for duty the way that Win had been. His brother had taken to responsibility like a duck to water, whereas Charles had reveled in his role as second son. It had freed him to follow his own inclinations. And even when those inclinations ultimately led to his being sent down from Oxford, his straitlaced father had given him the tongue-lashing he deserved but had not been overly outraged, for he had had Winfield to focus on as a point of pride. And after a few weeks of enduring Charles reluctant rustication, Lord Meredith had been more than happy to purchase a pair of colors and pack his younger son off to the Peninsula.

Charles had found his element in the army. The regiment satisfied two basic needs: adventure and companionship. As for a third need, he'd broken hearts from Vitoria all the way to Brussels. He would have been able to survive Napoleon's defeat well enough, he thought. Indeed, he had been looking forward to being billeted back to England. What he felt he could not survive was Winfield's death and the resulting responsibilities heaped upon his shoulders.

When the old gentleman bought him out, Charles had gone dutifully home to Gloucester, where he had tried for a time to assume the role of heir apparent. But after failing to live up to his brother's filial standards—at least as they had been recalled by a grieving father—Charles had abandoned the attempt. "Nothing's to be gained by us constantly locking horns, sir" had been the way he put it. "When I become Lord Meredith, I'll be it. In the meantime, you're doing it splendidly and don't need me in your hair. I'm off to London."

"What you ought to do is get married and settle down!" his sire had bellowed as they glared at one another across a library table.

"Well, the metropolis is as good a place as any to find a bride."

"Not where you're apt to look."

"Well, then, sir, for the sake of the continuation of the Danforth line, I'll look in at Almack's now and then and check on the latest crop of marriageable females. And in the meantime, to salve your disappointment in me, you might take comfort in the fact that no one wishes you a longer life and better health than I do.''

''I find no comfort in the fact that your chief aim in life is to shirk all responsibility,'' his father had replied.

And though several of His Majesty's higher-ranking officers, including the great Wellington himself, would certainly have taken emphatic exception to that remark, their opinion was of little comfort to Charles Danforth.

For the truth was, though Charles rarely allowed himself to admit it, he regretted being a grave disappointment to his father. And the fact that he couldn't get along with his sire for longer than twenty-four hours at a stretch had nothing to say to his regard for the crusty old gentleman.

He sighed heavily as he contemplated the pain that his latest scrape was going to cause his father. He hoped to heaven that word wouldn't reach his lordship till after the cross-country was run and everything was right and tight again. But gossipmongering being what it was, Lord Meredith probably already knew that his son was wanted by the law. The news might really kill him. He was nothing if not proud.

The port was making Charles maudlin. He found himself regretting that he hadn't tried harder to please his father. Perhaps if he'd kept his promise to look in at Almack's now and then, who knows, he might have lost his heart to some respectable heiress with a pedigree as ancient as his own who would have sent his father into transports. He was dreamily mulling over this unlikely fantasy when the knob on the chamber door began to turn.

George at last! Well, thank God for it. He needed a spot of company to shake him out of the doldrums.

It was not Lord Severn, however, who slipped inside and noiselessly closed the chamber door. And who was wearing a seductive smile, a robe of deep rose silk, and, unless Charles missed his guess, very little else.

''Why, hullo, Mrs. Alden.'' Captain Danforth tucked a straying end of his borrowed scarf underneath the collar of

George's dressing gown. "I must say that you're a sight for sore eyes." His smile was more than cordial. "The very ticket, in fact, to cure a near-fatal fit of the blue devils. Gwenny, my dear, do come in."

Chapter Ten

*L*ady Cassandra also had had difficulty falling asleep. She had finally abandoned the effort altogether and, lighting her candle, had picked up the copy of *Pride and Prejudice*, written by the unknown author of *Sense and Sensibility*, that she kept beside her bed. She had read the novel three times before, which perhaps explained why it now failed to hold her attention. Still, former repetitions had only added to her enjoyment. Perhaps it was that her own recent amorous adventures had made Elizabeth Bennet's exploits seem a bit tamer. At any rate, Cassandra was less than irritated when a soft knock sounded on her door. Even as she called, "Come in," Nan, an upstairs maid, had already done so.

Never noted for a cool head, sixteen-year-old Nan appeared more than ordinarily agitated as she stood in her nightgown with one bare foot placed atop another. "Oh, your ladyship," she wailed, "I didn't know what to do for the best, so I just ran down here to tell you. There's going to be the most awful row!"

"What on earth! Calm down, Nan. First take a deep breath. Then explain yourself."

The maid gasped obediently. "It's Mr. Parker, m'lady. He saw some woman slipping into that toffish valet's room. Lord Severn's man, I mean. The one what took Mr. Chesney's place."

The maid had Cassandra's full attention. She reached for the robe at the foot of her bed as Nan rushed through her narrative. "Katie and I share a room you know, ma'am." She paused for confirmation.

"Of course I know. Do go on."

"Well, Mr. Parker thinks Katie's much too forward with the gentlemen guests here, if you take my meaning." Her ruddy cheeks grew redder still. "And the last time Lord Devenham had guests, well, Mr. Parker accused Katie of visiting one of 'em in his chamber. She denied it, of course." Nan sniffed dubiously. "But Mr. Parker said if he ever caught her, she'd be out on her ear. And so, m'lady, when he saw this person in her nightclothes sneaking into Lord Severn's rooms, where that new valet sleeps, well, he put two and two together and come up with Katie. It was dark and all, and Mr. Parker can't see that well without his spectacles even in daylight and is too uppity to wear 'em while he's on duty. Well, anyhow, he came straight up to our room to see if Katie was in her bed, and of course she wasn't."

"Are you trying to tell me, Nan, that Katie is, er, visiting Lord Severn's Godfrey?"

"No, that's just what she's not doing, m'lady. She sneaked out to meet the second gardener. But I couldn't tell Mr. Parker that. Katie would murder me." She burst into tears.

For one humiliating moment, all Cassandra felt was profound relief that the overblown, loosely moraled Katie was not keeping a tryst with Godfrey. But her attention was recaptured as Nan blubbered on.

"I should've told on Katie, though," she wailed, "for Mr. Parker's gone to fetch Lord Devenham and also Lord Severn—on account of it being his man who's sinning—

and he's hoping to catch the two going at it, begging your ladyship's pardon. For Mr. Parker's ever so strict and moral and won't allow such goings-on in his household," she explained. "But, oh, m'lady, if it ain't Katie there with that Mr. Godfrey, well, then, it's got to be one of the female guests. And there's going to be an awful dustup when they all go barging in."

"Oh, dear heavens!" The full import of Nan's dire prediction dawned. Nor did Cassandra have to wonder just who the misbehaving guest might be. "You did say Parker is fetching my father?"

"Yes, your ladyship. And Lord Severn."

"Very well, then, Nan." Cassandra assumed a calm briskness she was far from feeling. "I'll take care of the situation. You can go back to your room." She poked her head out into the hall and, seeing that the coast was clear, motioned the maid to follow. "Go to bed, Nan. Now!" she whispered, noting that the servant, having shifted her awesome responsibility, seemed prone to await developments. "And, Nan, if you breathe one word of this to anybody—and that goes for Katie—well, your friend won't be the only maid in trouble. But thank you for telling me. It was the proper thing to do. Now scoot. Before Parker sees you in your nightdress and thinks the worst."

"Oh, lor', m'lady, surely he wouldn't!" A scarlet Nan ran barefoot down the hall while Cassandra hurried to her cousin's chamber where she rapped, none too softly, upon the door. There was no time to waste. She rattled the knob as a second warning. The door came open in her hand. Not only did the couple inside lack all proper moral restraint, they were wanting in sense as well! The very least they might have done was shove a heavy chest against the door. "Godfrey, are you there?" she hissed, entering with eyes averted.

"Why, yes, m'lady." Since the answering voice sounded more astonished than mortified, Cassandra risked a peek. Godfrey and Mrs. Alden sat propped against the headboard of the bed. So far, it would seem, the only thing they'd been enjoying was a glass of wine. But her father was not apt to stop and congratulate himself on this piece of luck. Finding his fiancée and a servant on such easy terms would be sufficient to bring on a coronary. It would not require that they be caught in *flagrante delicto*.

"Well, well, Godfrey." Mrs. Alden was not in the least embarrassed. As a matter of fact, she appeared a trifle up in the world, if not to say inebriated. "You do seem to attract more than your share of female company. Tell me, does this go on all night?"

"Oh, do be quiet!" Cassandra could not waste time with false civility. "I've come to warn you that the butler is bringing my father up here. So if you have any regard for your fiancé at all, run! And Godfrey"—she fairly blistered the valet with a look—"you be thinking of a story that will explain a female visitor. Or perhaps you have one ready. No doubt you're used to dealing with such emergencies."

Mrs. Alden, suddenly sober, was leaping off the bed and Godfrey was scrambling after her when the trio froze. The unmistakable sound of exaggerated stealth was heard approaching down the hall.

"Oh, my God," Mrs. Alden whispered, turning pale.

"Oh, hell!" the valet swore beneath his breath.

"Quick, under here!" Cassandra gave her future stepmother a shove that sent her scrambling underneath the floor-length curtains of the bed.

A second later, when the ad hoc committee for moral decency entered, with Parker holding the door, Lord Devenham striding inside, and Lord Severn lagging behind, it was to find Lady Cassandra in a singularly chaste-looking robe and nightcap seated by the empty Adam fireplace sipping a glass of port. Charles, although rather raffishly attired in a rich brocade dressing gown that stopped inches short of its intended floor length and left his ankles bare, still managed the well-trained servant's detached decorum as he replaced the wine decanter on its silver tray.

"Cassandra!" Devenham's shocked voice shattered a stunned silence. At this moment it was difficult to ascertain whether the earl would—or could—have been any more horrified had he been aware that his fiancée lay quailing and quaking underneath the bed. But his shock, great as it was, was no match for Parker's. The majordomo clutched at his heart and, for the first time since he'd entered domestic service as a mere lad, so far forgot himself as to sink into a chair in the presence of the gentry. "Oh, my word" was the Viscount Severn's feeble contribution to the scene.

"Cassandra, explain yourself!" Lord Devenham's wrath was terrible to behold. It lacked only a flaming sword as the final touch. "Explain yourself, I say! If indeed there can be an explanation for your indelicate—no, by gad, your *indecent* conduct."

Cassandra's eyebrows rose. "Aren't you coming it a bit strong, Papa? It seems more to the point to inquire what you and Parker are doing here. But never mind that now," she amended hastily as her father's purple hue increased alarmingly. "As to what I'm doing, that should be quite evident. Waiting for George, of course."

The viscount emitted a strangling sound.

"Oh, er, will that be all, m'lady?" Charles, receiving a wave of dismissal in answer to his murmur, withdrew into the dressing room where he wiped his brow with a brocade sleeve.

"Waiting for George!" The earl's voice increased both in indignation and volume. "Dressed like a—like a lightskirt! Don't care if he is your cousin. I tell you, it won't do!"

"Whyever not?"

"My God, girl, you have to ask?" Devenham's tone changed suddenly from righteous indignation to pain. "I don't know what's come over you, Cassie. I vow I don't. Such hoydenish behavior ain't like you at all. Last person I'd ever expect to behave like some kind of trollop."

"Well, really, Father. Your behavior seems to be the thing in question here. This Cheltenham tragedy you're enacting is entirely out of place. You seem to forget that George and I are betrothed."

The viscount's choking intensified, as if the amount of

squeeze of an invisible noose was slowly being stepped up.

"Not officially you ain't! Besides, being betrothed don't give you leave—"

"Oh, does it not?" The daughter gave the father a speaking look. "I have it, by the highest precept and example, that engaged couples do indeed visit one another in their chambers late at night."

It was quite impossible for the earl's color to intensify. He did, however, contrive to look quite sheepish. "The cases ain't the same at all," he blustered.

"Oh, are they not? I fail to see a distinction."

"Well, there is one. If a betrothed couple is older and has been married before . . . Besides—"

"Well, I should not have thought that such technicalities would affect the proprieties. But," she said with a shrug, "if you say so."

"I do say so." Devenham was regaining some composure. "And that's not all I have to say. If this is the kind of rackety behavior I can expect from you, well then I intend to send a notice to the *Gazette* immediately. Society had best learn of your betrothal while you still have a shred of character left!"

"Arrggh!" The strangling had reached the terminal stage. "Oh, I say, do stand up, there's a good fellow, Parker."

The butler managed to vacate the imitation bamboo armchair barely in time for an ashen Viscount Severn to collapse upon it.

Chapter Eleven

"What I quite fail to understand is why you did it. You had a perfect opportunity to be rid of me. And you'll not convince me you're pleased at the prospect of having me for a mama-in-law."

Cassandra had returned from her morning ride to find Mrs. Alden waiting in her bedchamber. The lady's thanks for the previous night's deliverance had been profuse.

"My feelings have nothing to say in the matter," Cassandra replied, removing her riding hat and sitting on the window seat next to her visitor. Mrs. Alden had brought along some handwork and showed no intention of moving on. "My father dotes on you. I should not like to see him hurt."

"And I dote on him and should not like to hurt him." Gwendolen did not miss the other's skepticism. "You doubt that, I can see. Well, I suppose it's understandable. But the fact is, you refine too much on last night's, uh, episode. Oh, I grant you, it did not look well. That's why I'm so grateful that you saved me from being caught out by your father. For I fear that he, like you, would think the worst. But the thing is"—Mrs. Alden now tried to give a "first time" illusion to a speech she'd been rehearsing all night long,—"Godfrey and I have known each other for donkey's years. His father was our butler. And since I was a solitary child, we shared a nursery together. It was an unorthodox arrangement, that I grant you, but my father was well known as an eccentric."

If Cassandra thought privately that Mrs. Alden would have graduated to the schoolroom before Godfrey was in the nursery, she refrained from saying so.

"So I was delighted to find him here," the other woman continued, "and eager to discuss old times and to hear the latest news of his dear, dear father. Ours is not the usual servant-mistress relationship at all, you see."

"So I observed," Cassandra offered dryly. "And while your democratic sentiments might do you credit in places like America and France, you cannot expect my father to share them."

"I know. I know. That, too, was why I was anxious to talk to Godfrey. I have requested him to maintain a proper distance should we meet in company. He assures me that he will be most circumspect. But now I want to find a way to express my gratitude to you."

"Oh, but that isn't necessary."

"Oh, but it is. I wish us to be close friends. And I have thought of one service I could perform. I—"

"Oh, so have I!" Cassandra interrupted her, having just had a brainstorm. "The kindest thing you could do for me is to persuade Papa not to send a notice to the *Gazette*."

"Oh, dear. That was not what I had in mind. And, frankly, what you ask may not be easy. I'm afraid he was most shocked by the apparent intimacy between you and Lord Severn. His greatest wish now is to put the seal of propriety on what he calls your 'outrageous behavior.' "

"I know he does. But the last thing I wished to do was land poor George in such a coil."

"Oh? I had thought perhaps you'd done so deliberately."

"Indeed not!" Cassandra was indignant. "I would never trap someone into marriage."

"No, I can see that." Her appraisal of Cassandra's unfashionable riding costume and hairstyle spoke for itself. "But I had thought that perhaps you were not actually averse to the idea of marrying Lord Severn. Many would consider him quite a catch. His fortune is considerable, is it not? And he appears to be the soul of amiability."

"It is, and he is," Cassandra agreed. "But not only have I no desire to wed my cousin George, you must have heard his collapse when my father decided to announce our betrothal."

"It did put George into quite a taking." Mrs. Alden smiled.

"Yes, it did, poor lamb. And I cannot bear for him to be made to suffer for my—and your—impetuosity."

"Your point is well taken." Mrs. Alden sighed. "And since, as you've been at pains to indicate, I'm most to blame for George's plight, I'll do my utmost to bring Devenham around. The best course of action, perhaps," she mused aloud, "is to hold him to his promise to give some other suitors a chance to win you. After all, Devenham is not exactly in raptures over the prospect of Severn for a son. I shall point out that Mr. Davies, for one, is in love with you. And have you noticed that Sir Champion Pue is growing quite attentive?"

"I most certainly have not!" Cassandra exclaimed.

"That's because you are quite backward—if you'll forgive my frankness—when it comes to recognizing flirts. Yes, I shall quite insist that you be given the chance to shop around a bit before your father bestows your hand on the first suitor in line for it. I shall point out," she said, grinning wickedly, "that he can always ensure your propriety by locking you in your room."

"Or, better yet, by letting me set up my own household."

"That's just what he'll not do." Mrs. Alden frowned

down at her tambouring. "No, m'dear, I fear that last night will only make him more determined to see you safely wed. And I confess that I'm in complete agreement with him on that point."

"Well, I must say you disappoint me. I had thought that you, as an independent woman of the world, would see my point."

"Me? Independent? Nonsense. I am a woman of the world enough, however, to recognize the enormous advantages of being married. I speak not only of the financial advantage, but of the social. Why a married woman may do as she pleases, whereas a single one is constantly beset on all sides by taboos," Mrs. Alden explained. "If it's independence you want, my dear, well, you'd best marry for it. And I intend to help you."

"How?" There was more suspicion than eagerness in the question, with perhaps the slightest seasoning of hostility as well.

"To begin with, I'm going to lend you Annette, my maid. And you must give her carte blanche to do what she likes with your hair and wardrobe. Annette will make you outwardly presentable. I myself will try to instill a few of the graces required to make oneself agreeable to the other sex."

"Isn't there some contradiction here?" Cassandra tried to hold her ground. "You have just implied that two gentlemen are in love with me already. That being the case, won't you and Annette be going to a lot of trouble for nothing? Or worse. A new me might put them off entirely."

"Indeed not. A great gulf lies between attracting a gentleman like Sir Champion and being able to fix his interest. And as for Mr. Davies, well, the most flaming passion is soon cooled by being pushed into the mud."

"He did bring it upon himself," Cassandra muttered defensively.

"No doubt. Plumb, alas, is inclined to be impetuous. But there are ways of discouraging such overfamiliarity, my dear, without actual brawling."

"Oh, I'm sure your more accomplished flirt would have simply said, 'Oh, la, Mr. Davies, sir!' and rapped his knuckles playfully with her fan. Then all would have been instantaneous decorum. But, frankly, such a course never occurred to me. And, furthermore—I might just as well go ahead and say it—I've no desire to fix Mr. Davies's interest with me."

Mrs. Alden shook her head sadly. "My dear Cassandra, I am sorry to hear you say so. For, frankly, I was hoping that you would return his regard. You see, I hold Mr. Davies in the highest esteem, as I feel you will grow to do if you allow yourself to get to know him. Plumb and I have been the greatest of friends for years and—"

"Was he perhaps in the nursery with you and Godfrey?" Cassandra interrupted.

"Why, no, of course not. Plumb is quite— Oh!" Gwendolen laughed her tinkly laugh. "But you're bamming me, of course. How really droll. But as I was saying, I think if you give yourself a chance to know Mr. Davies better and show your father, by more attention to your appearance and behavior, that you wish to consider other suitors before settling for Severn, one of two things could happen."

"Indeed?"

"Most likely you'll end up by falling in love with Plumb. But if that should not happen, you will at least have gained some time. And who knows, stranger things have happened, perhaps your father will eventually come 'round and allow you to live independently. The alternative is, of course, to do nothing at all and let your father send his notice to the *Gazette*."

"Ring for Annette." Cassandra capitulated.

As it developed, acquiring a new persona was not as tedious as Cassandra had anticipated. She became quite fascinated, in fact, by the artful snipping Annette was doing to her hair and could not believe the transformation the Frenchwoman was able to make in her five-year-old evening gown. After a ruthless reduction of trimmings and an almost scandalous lowering of the neckline, Annette pronounced the gown quite *à la mode*—at least for Hampshire.

True, being forced to pore for hours over pattern books and to weigh the merits of various materials, only to have her opinions instantly overruled by Mrs. Alden, Annette, and the village dressmaker, did grow quite tiresome. But that evening as Cassandra stood in front of the glass, a finished product, she decided that all the fuss had actually been worth it. "I do look better," she conceded.

Annette threw up her hands at such typical English understatement. " 'Better'! M'lady is transformed! Thanks to me, you will turn every masculine head and break the hearts both left and right."

Cassandra was still smiling at such typical Gallic exaggeration as she left her chamber to go down to dinner at the precise same moment Charles emerged from his. Not only did the valet's head turn, as predicted, but his chin dropped as well. "My word! What have you done to yourself?"

"Godfrey, are you addressing me?" her ladyship inquired with frosty hauteur.

"Beg pardon, m'lady. I got carried away. May I say that you look absolutely stunning?"

"Well, you just did, I suppose. Godfrey, are you certain you're not Irish?" Cassandra was doing her best to sound withering, but it was obvious that she welcomed the fulsome compliment.

"One-hundred-percent English. And I haven't done you justice. Of course, you may recall that I did predict a lot could be done for your appearance if you'd only take the trouble. But even I did not expect you to turn into a diamond of the first water. Rather goes to show, now, doesn't it?"

"Goes to show what, Godfrey?"

"Just how much artifice is involved in a female's looks. We poor men never really know just what hit us, do we?" Charles told her.

"Speaking of artifice"—she felt it time to change the subject—"I see you're wearing your sling again. I should think, Godfrey, that the case history of your broken arm would be of great interest to medical science. It's quite wonderful how well it is at times. Last night might serve as an example. Do you suppose the others observed that you were slingless then?''

"Well, you see, m'lady, my arm had improved amazingly. But last night put a terrible strain on my whole constitution. And I'm afraid my poor bone relapsed.''

Cassandra snorted.

"Please don't do that, m'lady.'' The valet frowned. "If I may be allowed to say so, that method of showing disapproval is at complete odds with your new appearance. A mild 'Fiddlesticks,' for example, would be a much more feminine expression of skepticism.''

Cassandra had an expression on the tip of her tongue designed to singe the valet's eyebrows when another door opened down the hall.

"Very good, m'lady.'' Charles's bow was a model of subservience. But the laughter in his eyes at her frustration at not being allowed to deliver her scathing setdown was not. "I will give Lord Severn your message,'' he improvised, in case the elderly couple waiting for Cassandra might be curious. Her ladyship had no choice but to stifle her fury and join her Devon cousins.

Her good humor was partly restored, however, by their simultaneous reactions. "What a picture you make!'' "How lovely you look, my dear.'' Then at the foot of the stairs, her father's expression added the final fillip to her self-esteem. "My word, Cassie, is that really you?''

She was not quite so pleased, however, by the effect her altered appearance had on Mr. Davies. All during dinner he persisted in showering her with compliments to the point of embarrassment. And when he actually invited her to stroll outside with him, her face must have reflected her opinion of that suggestion, for he hastened to plead for the chance to redeem himself and to prove he could behave like a gentleman. It was not Mr. Davies's powers of persuasion that won the day, however, but Cassandra's promise to give Mrs. Alden's friend another chance. Besides, she owed it to poor George to play the field. Reluctantly she agreed.

"Poor George," however, who had overheard the invitation from across the table, elected to go along. Nor could all of Mr. Davies's pointed remarks about the awkwardness of a threesome dissuade him.

George himself was frankly at a loss as to why he'd suddenly elected to chaperon his cousin when his expressed desire had been to fling Cassandra at Plumb Davies's head. Perhaps his conscience had belatedly reminded him of Davies's unsavory reputation. And he certainly could not expect his unsophisticated cousin to know how to deal with an experienced rake. Or perhaps it was his own good name he was concerned with. For should he become Cassandra's husband—a fate he felt himself being pushed toward with the inexorableness of an old Greek tragedy—he didn't want the gossipmongers chewing on his wife's past association with a here-and-thereian. But whatever George's true motive for his snap decision to guard his cousin like a good Dutch uncle might have been, he was candid enough to recognize that the fact Cassandra was in amazing good looks, by Jove, had made his chivalrous decision a great deal easier.

Plumb Davies was no callow youth. It was not in his nature to pout when thwarted. He was wont instead to cut his losses and to take advantage of whatever opportunities a change of plan might offer. And so, as the trio set forth on their evening walk, Mr. Davies exerted himself to charm not only Lady Cassandra but her intrusive cousin George as well. And if the latter seemed to regard the effort with more suspicion than delight, well, Mr. Davies was more amused than annoyed by this wary attitude.

Gradually, however, Lord Severn seemed to relax under the combined influence of Plumb's amusing anecdotes, the scent of roses, and Lady Cassandra's tossing curls. Davies felt the time was ripe to prise the information out of him that Gwenny had, so far, failed to extract from Charles Danforth. He maneuvered the talk to the upcoming steeplechase.

"I've entered Thunderer," he offered, as if he thought

this would be news to George. "How about you, Severn? Do you plan to ride?"

George was not so far under the other's spell that he failed to revert to his former suspicion. "I ain't decided," he said dismissively, pausing on the stone path to inspect a rosebush as though looking among the blossoms for a new topic of conversation.

But Mr. Davies allowed no opening. "Better make up your mind, old man. The field's almost full, I understand. Though I did hear they're holding a few places open for latecomers—which is odd, to say the least. Come to think on it, you don't suppose the promoters are still hoping your friend Danforth will enter, do you?"

"Don't see how he could. Gone to France, you know."

"Oh, yes. So I heard. Do you have any idea what he might have done with his horse?"

George had little talent for dissimulation. "Charlie must have taken the horse with him," he said uneasily. "Bound to have, I should think. Charlie ain't likely to be parted from that animal." They walked on, three abreast.

"Well, no doubt you're right. You do know him better than anyone. Still, it had occurred to me that you might be keeping his horse for him," Plumb said.

"Me? Oh, no. Probably took it with him, just like I said. Or could have left him at Tattersall's, I suppose."

"As a matter of fact, he didn't. I checked there before I left London."

"That was a deuced odd thing for you to do."

"Not so odd when you come to think on it. Let's just call it a reasonable precaution. Why, I even had a look in the stables here today, thinking, wrongly, I now see, that you might have brought the horse down here with you, George. Can't blame a man for making sure. Without Danforth and his stallion in the race, you see, I am the odds-on favorite. Oh, I still think my horse and I have an excellent chance of beating Danforth's stallion, even with him on it. But being quite prudent by nature, I don't like to place my wagers till I'm sure of the field."

The trio had reached the wooden bridge and crossed it

single file, each pursuing his or her own thoughts. But when they closed ranks again, Cassandra, who had been obeying Mrs. Alden's instructions concerning male-oriented conversations, could contain herself no longer. "What race are you talking about?" she blurted out.

Mr. Davies turned to her in surprise. "I can't believe you don't already know, given your equestrian passion."

"Oh, I can take horses or leave them alone." She said this airily, à la Mrs. Alden. Then, rather more naturally, "No, I don't know anything about it. And if there's a race being run, I can't understand why Papa hasn't mentioned it."

"Probably had more pressing matters to occupy him." Mr. Davies smiled. "His upcoming nuptials must have wiped all else from his mind."

"Probably didn't want you to know," George offered with rather more accuracy than Mr. Davies. "Made it plain he wants your mind on other things than horses."

Cassandra opened her mouth to express just what she thought of her father's duplicity. Then, mindful of the analogy Gwendolen Alden had drawn between the attraction properties of vinegar and honey, she closed it with a snap. Her smile came perilously close to becoming a simper. "Ooh, Mr. Davies," Cassandra cooed, as her cousin looked suspicious. "Do you really plan to race? It's too thrilling for words. But isn't it dreadfully dangerous?"

Plumb Davies did not hesitate to enlarge his heroic image. While pooh-poohing the danger, he went on to describe the steeplechase terrain as the "worst imaginable" and to list all the various types of hazards the rider would encounter.

"There! It is dangerous. Did I not say so? Whyever would so many gentlemen risk life and limb in such a perilous undertaking?" she asked.

"For the sport of it."

"Or the money," the viscount opined drily.

"Touché." Mr. Davies refused to take offense. "Though still standing by my answer, I will agree that the money serves as a great incentive."

"Oh, really?" Cassandra dropped her missishness. "Is the prize large, then?"

Mr. Davies smiled at such naïveté. "It's the wagering your cousin refers to. That's what makes the endeavor financially worthwhile. Mark my words, Lady Cassandra, fortunes will be made and lost at Lower Wallop. And that, my dear viscount"—he bowed to George—"is really what I meant when I referred to the sport of racing. Much as I love the thrill of the ride, I must admit that backing a favorite or putting one's blunt down on a long shot gives a different but no less satisfying thrill."

"You did say that fortunes could be won in the betting?" she asked.

"Yes, he did say that." George looked uneasily at his cousin's thoughtful expression. "He also mentioned that fortunes could be lost."

"Oh, don't be so dampening, Lord Severn. As for you, m'lady, you must promise that you'll come to Lower Wallop to see me ride. And what is more, you must wager in order to make the race more interesting. Forgive my apparent immodesty, but barring last-minute surprises, I am the favorite. So if you'll put a few pounds on Thunderer to win, well, I can assure you you won't be sorry. Do say you'll come, Lady Cassandra."

Her ladyship, however, appeared to have lost interest in the subject as quickly as she'd gained it. She had paused to pull a dead blossom off a rosebush and was staring at it absently. Mr. Davies removed it gently from her hand and substituted a dark crimson, half-opened bud that he had plucked. "Watch out for thorns" was the viscount's advice as Cassandra slowly rotated the flower by its stem, her mind seemingly miles away.

"Come now, Lady Cassandra," Mr. Davies chided. "I do believe you've gone woolgathering and haven't heard a word I've said."

She looked up at him then, quite seriously. "Oh, no, I assure you, sir, you much mistake the matter. I have been listening quite intently."

"Well, then, I am glad to hear it. But you have not told me yet if you will come to see me ride."

"Oh, did I not answer? Then you are right, sir, I was woolgathering. Pray do forgive me. And be assured of one thing. I have every intention of going to the steeplechase at Lower Wallop."

Chapter Twelve

A few mornings later, Cassandra arose especially early. She carried a spyglass with her as she set forth on her ride. She was counting on a repetition of the rather peculiar activity she had glimpsed on several occasions and now intended to observe more particularly without allowing herself to be observed in return.

Since the day she had encountered George's valet out riding and they had raced, Cassandra had been aware that he had continued the early-morning exercise. And she suspected that he had been at pains to avoid her, just as she had contrived to stay away from him. Even so, she had from time to time observed Godfrey from a distance and thought his conduct eccentric, to say the least.

This morning she deliberately rode in the direction she had previously seen him take, and as she topped a grassy rise, she sighted a horse and rider galloping away from her in a distant meadow. Cassandra pulled Pegasus to a halt and brought the spyglass to her eye, adjusting it in time to see the stallion clear a hedgerow in a graceful arc. The white horse sped across a newly plowed field, splashed through a rocky brook, jumped a ditch, whirled unexpectedly, and headed back her way. Cassandra held her ground while he jumped the hedgerow from the other side. Then, just as she was about to close her telescope and leave, the rider stood up in the stirrups, lifted his hat, and bowed. The spyglass brought a cocky smile uncomfortably into focus.

"Oh, botheration!" Lady Cassandra's first impulse, as Charles headed her way, was to turn Pegasus and gallop home. But having been caught red-handed, it somehow seemed unsporting. She stayed.

"Good morning, your ladyship." Whether caught slipping into windows in the dead of night, discovered in bed with a nobleman's fiancée, or under covert and shameless observation, the valet never seemed to lose his jaunty aplomb. Cassandra noted this fact with more than a touch of envy. She was feeling decidedly ill at ease.

"Practicing to be one of His Majesty's spies, then, are we?" He nodded at the telescope she still held.

"Hardly. I often take this along when I'm out riding. I like to observe the wildlife I encounter."

"Oh, I see." From his knowing grin, he obviously did see. He dropped Trafalgar's bridle.

"And when I accidentally trained my glass on you, I could not help but become curious about what you were doing." Cassandra also gave her mount the chance to graze.

"Begging your ladyship's pardon, I can't see why. I mentioned that I ride most mornings."

"Yes, but it's your choice of route that made me curious. You certainly shun the obvious bridle paths."

"Oh, well, now, there's a good reason for that." He paused a moment to think of one. "Seeing as how I promised that you'd not know I was on the place and knowing as I do how your ladyship likes to ride out early, well, I was doing my best to keep out of sight. I had no way of knowing that I'd be focused in your glass like all the other wildlife, now, did I?"

"I'm sorry to hear, Godfrey, that I'm the unwitting cause of your pushing your poor mount over such a rigorous terrain."

"Oh, that's quite all right, ma'am. Trafalgar loves a challenge," he replied.

"Fustian! Do you know what I think, Godfrey?"

"Oh, no, your ladyship. I've never been able to get the faintest clue to that."

"I think that all your hedge-jumping and stream-fording has nothing to do with avoiding me. I think it concerns the Lower Wallop Steeplechase. Tell me, do you plan to run there?"

"How could I, your ladyship? That's a race for gentlemen."

"Oh." The wind left Cassandra's sails. "I didn't think of that."

The two horses suddenly drew together to compete for the same succulent patch of clover. As her riding skirt brushed Charles thigh, Cassandra gave Pegasus a jerk to separate them.

The valet tactfully overlooked the gesture. "But I will confess that you were nearly on the right track about that race m'lady. I was wondering just how well Trafalgar here might do in that kind of competition. He's a remarkable animal, if I do say so."

"Oh, I agree," she replied, from a two-foot distance. "And frankly it's a shame that he's discriminated against that way. It does seem that the horse's pedigree should count and not the rider's."

"Oh, well. You can see their point if you think on it. It wouldn't do for ordinary folk to discover that the upper class ain't that superior after all. Which might well happen if just any old ragtag and bobtail was allowed to enter in their race."

"That's quite enough of that sort of talk!"

"Beg pardon, m'lady. I did forget myself."

"Very well. Just don't do it again." She mused for a moment. "Perhaps you could persuade my cousin George to ride Trafalgar."

"I said Trafalgar's remarkable, m'lady. I didn't say that he was supernatural."

"Well, yes, I do see what you mean." She patted Pegasus absently while the two animals edged closer again. "Tell me, what do you know of Mr. Davies's equestrian skill?"

"I beg your pardon?"

"Oh, don't pretend ignorance, Godfrey. It won't wash. Anyone on such intimate terms with Mrs. Alden is bound to know a great deal about Mr. Davies."

"Oh, I wouldn't go so far as to say Mrs. Alden and I are 'intimate.' "

Cassandra barely restrained herself from snorting. He noted the effort and repressed a grin. "I'd hardly know what else to call it. Furthermore, I must say that the fact you two shared a nursery hardly excuses—"

"Beg pardon, m'lady?" he interrupted.

"Mrs. Alden has told me how the two of you were raised like brother and sister and shared a nursery. But I should not have to point out that such a peculiar circumstance hardly excuses your shocking behavior. And, believe me, my father, if he should learn of it, would not be likely to take the matter lightly. But I did not intend to refer to that. Indeed, I am doing my best to forget the incident ever happened. Pegasus!" Her face flamed as she was wedged against the valet's thigh once more. "The hillside's covered with grass! You don't have to have Trafalgar's mouthful!"

"Like children, ain't they," her companion commented as she widened the gap between them again. "But before you do forget that incident we were talking about, ma'am, let me assure you that such a thing won't happen again."

"I do not require your assurance, Godfrey. In the future Mrs. Alden plans to treat you in the manner dictated by the difference in your social classes. So let us drop the subject."

"Gladly, m'lady."

"What I was hoping to discuss was Mr. Davies."

"If you insist." He sighed. "Though, frankly, that subject doesn't rate much higher with me than the one we just abandoned. Are you sure you want to talk about Mr. Davies? If so, couldn't we dismount? The discussion may give me a sudden queasy turn."

He was out of the saddle and reaching up to help her down before she could agree or disagree. Then his strong hands around her waist held her speechless for a moment longer. But after he'd guided her over to sit on the moss underneath a mulberry tree, she looked up at him curiously.

"Well, you are nothing if not contradictory, Godfrey. The other evening in my room"—she colored as she dredged up one more taboo subject—"you spoke very highly of Mr. Davies. Now you're belittling him. Needless to say, I'm quite confused."

"No more than I am," he admitted. "I can't explain it myself. Except that at the time I thought any marriage was preferable to the daft scheme you had in mind for your life. But now that I know you better, the idea of you marrying Plumb Davies is unthinkable. The man's a gazetted fortune hunter."

"Thank you for your concern, but I've no intention of marrying Mr. Davies. My only interest in him is in his riding skill. He tells me he's good. Is he?"

The valet had removed his hat. Cassandra thought it looked familiar and went on to notice that he had acquired some proper, if ill-fitting, riding clothes that looked suspiciously like castoffs of her father's. She was even further distracted as the breeze ruffled his dark, sweat-dampened hair.

"I can't fault Mr. Davies as a rider."

"I beg your pardon?" She jerked her mind back to the issue at hand.

"I said that I can't fault Mr. Davies when it comes to riding." His tone implied that this was the only area so restricted.

"And what about his horse?" Cassandra asked.

"Thunderer? A prime goer, no mistake."

"I see. Well, Mr. Davies has been urging me to place

a wager on him to win the Lower Wallop Steeplechase. What do you think his chances are?''

The valet shrugged. "I wouldn't like to say, your ladyship. The odds would seem to favor Mr. Davies. But then the field ain't complete yet. And even if it were . . . Well, anything can happen in a horse race. That's why they call it gambling.''

"I'm aware of all that, Godfrey," she said impatiently. "I merely want your assessment of Mr. Davies's skill and his horse's ability.''

"Well, since you insist, I'd say go ahead and place a small wager if you like. But I wouldn't risk the family jewels if I were you. Thunderer can be beaten.''

"Ahhh," she breathed, her eyes alight. "Now tell me. Could Trafalgar there, for instance, beat him?''

"I just explained—''

"I know Trafalgar's not racing," she said, stopping him. "We're speaking hypothetically. Could Trafalgar beat Thunderer?''

"In a breeze.''

"Ahhh," she repeated, smiling thoughtfully. She sat for a moment mulling over the conversation, then recollected herself and scrambled to her feet. "I must be getting back. Go on with what you were doing before I interrupted." They strolled together toward the horses that had cropped their way a distance down the hill. "Oh, by the by . . ." She broke the rather awkward silence. "I see you are again to be congratulated. No sling today.''

"No, I'm entirely healed now, I believe.''

"I do hope that doesn't mean you're going back to valeting. George's appearance has improved a thousandfold during your convalescence. I'd hate to see him backslide.''

"I think his lordship is more than happy with Mr. Davies's man, m'lady, and won't require my services in that capacity.''

"And I'd give a monkey to know in just what capacity you do serve him. You're most mysterious, Godfrey.''

"If you say so, m'lady.''

"I still think that George has lost a wager of some kind.

His cronies at Watier's club will gamble on anything. I know for a fact that George once wagered that a friend of his couldn't go a fortnight without eating prawns.''

''And did he win?''

''I couldn't say. But I'm convinced that someone's bet him that he couldn't put up with you in place of Chesney.''

''Well, that's an interesting theory, m'lady, but not one I should discuss.'' The valet captured Pegasus's bridle and pulled the horse around. ''Here, allow me to help you mount.''

''Oh, that isn't necessary.''

''Begging your pardon again, m'lady, but it's a habit you really should develop. A gentleman needs to feel depended on.''

''How ridiculous.'' She did not resist, however, when he once again placed his hands upon her waist.

But then the valet made no further move to assist the lady. He simply stood stock-still, staring down at her, his hands warm on her waist. He appeared bemused.

''What *is* the matter, Godfrey?''

''Surely you must know,'' he muttered. Then, as if against his will, he pulled her close and bent down to kiss her.

This time there was no question of reflex action, as had been the case when Charles Danforth had left Lady Cassandra's bedchamber in the wee hours of the night. For the evidence had been strong in that casual, brief encounter that any further experimentation of a similar nature could be fraught with peril. His every instinct cried out that this very unorthodox female, hovering on the brink of spinsterhood, could pose an even greater threat to his cherished freedom than Mr. Jeremy Gifford of Bow Street.

But Charles seemed unable to stop himself. He met the danger with his eyes wide open, in the figurative sense at any rate. And if in his heart of hearts he'd hoped that this second encounter with Lady Cassandra's lips would prove a decided letdown and allow him to discover that memory had exaggerated their sweetness and the intensity of the flame that they ignited within him, he was doomed to disappointment. If anything, he had been prone to downplay both effects.

Finally, slowly, reluctantly, he released her. Then he stepped back to await the repercussions. The Honorable Charles Danforth was prepared for almost anything, from a slap on the face to having a peal rung over him. But except for a slight, betraying flush, Lady Cassandra seemed quite self-possessed. "I knew I should have mounted unassisted" was her only comment, made while she did just that. But before she could ride away, he grabbed her reins.

"I ought not to have done that." His voice sounded rather hollow.

"That goes without saying. We both know that. But no need to put yourself into a taking over it. This time I share the blame."

"You do?" He seemed not to be able to credit what he'd just heard.

"Well, I'll have to, won't I?" she retorted. "For this time your action was not totally unexpected. And I did nothing to prevent it. You must surely realize that if I was capable of interrupting Mr. Davies's demonstration of ardor, I could certainly have done the same with you. And as I did not, I have to share the blame. So think no more of it, Godfrey."

"By God, you're cool!" He was growing a bit nettled. "And may I ask just why you didn't resist, m'lady?"

"Let's just say this was in the nature of an experiment."

"What sort of experiment?"

"Now *that* you may not ask." She dug her heels into Pegasus with a suddenness that caused the horse to jerk the reins from the valet's hand.

"Carry on as you were, Godfrey," Lady Cassandra called back across her shoulder as she galloped away.

"I damn well mean to try," Captain Danforth muttered grimly as, through narrowed eyes, he watched her speed recklessly down the hillside with not so much as a backward glance.

Chapter Thirteen

*L*ord Devenham, *a man of action and early hours, had* called upon his fiancée before that lady's dresser had had time to ply her arts. Mrs. Alden was propped up in bed sipping chocolate while doing her best to look pleased at having been awakened before ten o'clock.

Devenham had plopped down in an armchair that afforded a good view of his bride-to-be. That view was not flattering. "She's older than I thought" crept unbidden into his mind. He hastily tried to convince himself that, given his own maturity, Mrs. Alden's extra years were entirely to the good.

"Can't thank you enough for what you did for Cassie," his lordship repeated for the third—or possibly even the fourth—time.

"It was my pleasure." Mrs. Alden smiled wanly across the chocolate.

"Amazing what the right clothes and proper hairstyle can do. Had no idea the girl could look like that."

"Your daughter's a beauty, sir."

"No. That's doing it up too brown. But, by Jove, she did look quite the thing last night. Wish you could have got hold of her five years ago."

"Before her come-out? Oh, but think of the comfort she's brought you in the meantime. And it's certainly not too late."

"You're right, by Jove, and that's what I want to talk to you about. Would your nose be out of joint, Gwenny, if I was to go ahead and give Severn permission to marry Cassie?"

Mrs. Alden set her cup down carefully on the bed before replying. "La, why should I be upset? It is Cassandra you should consider. I think she only accepted Lord Severn to please you."

"I know that." Lord Devenham rose from his chair and began to pace about the room. "And George ain't the man I'd have chosen out of a large field. But then we don't have that kind of field. There's just him and your friend Davies."

"Ah, yes, Plumb."

"And the thing is, Gwenny—don't wish to speak ill of any bosom bow of yours—but the fact of the matter is, I can't like the fellow." He saw the hurt look on her face and quickly amended, "That is, I mean to say, I can't quite like him as a husband for my Cassie."

"He is a good deal older, of course. But still—"

"Oh, it ain't that. Good thing, actually, when the man's a bit more mature. It's just that . . . Well, I can't quite put my finger on it. But for one thing, the fellow's got too much town bronze for Cassie. She's a country girl."

"That's true. But she'd soon grow more sophisticated."

"I ain't so sure I want her to."

"I see. But then you're forgetting that Mr. Davies and Cassandra do share a consuming passion."

"I beg your pardon?" Lord Devenham only lacked a quizzing glass to complete his starchiness.

Mrs. Alden laughed her tinkly laugh. "Oh, don't put yourself into a taking, Devenham. I refer to their passion for horseflesh. Many a successful marriage has been built on less mutual interest than that.''

"Well, that's true, I suppose." He sounded rather unconvinced as he collapsed once more into the chair.

"And, if I do not mistake the matter, it's an interest that Lord Severn does not share."

"No, you ain't mistaken. George is completely cow-handed when it comes to handling a pair. As for hunting, the only person who likes that sport less than George is, just possibly, the fox."

"There now, you see."

"I'm not sure I do. Oh, I grant you, I'm not making sense. But I still think Cassie would deal better with George than she would with Davies. For one thing, same background. Cousins, you know. For another"—he looked uncomfortable—"I don't know how much you actually know about Plumb Davies, m'dear, but I keep hearing—and from more than one of my guests here—that the man's a gamester."

Again Mrs. Alden laughed. "Oh, my heavens, Devenham, that is not exactly damning news. Do you number any among your acquaintanceship who are not?"

"Don't think you take my meaning, Gwendolen. What I'm trying to say is, that's *all* he is. It's how he makes his living."

"What a rapper!" She dismissed the idea scornfully.

"Are you sure, m'dear? What do you actually know of the fellow's background?"

"Well, for one thing, he went to Eton and Oxford."

His lordship snorted, and it became immediately evident to Mrs. Alden where Lady Cassandra had acquired that unbecoming habit. Her version, however, was a pale copy of the derision Devenham expressed. "Eton and Oxford, eh? Well, a lot of scoundrels can make that claim."

Mrs. Alden chose to ignore this bit of editorializing. "And as to how Plumb lives, I've certainly never asked, but I believe he has a competency from an uncle in the north."

"Well, maybe that's so. Still, he can't be as plump in

the pocket as George is. No, the more I think on it, I'm convinced I should go ahead and notify the *Gazette*.''

''Oh, dear.'' His fiancée pouted prettily. Or tried to. Again, his lordship had the unworthy thought that she looked better by candlelight. The bright sunshine streaming in between the damask draperies was not flattering. ''I must go ahead and admit it. I am no different from any other scheming mama. I was hoping that Cassandra and Plumb would make a match of it. He's like the brother I never had, you see. So could you not, for my sake, dear Devenham, postpone your decision till you've had a chance to get to know him a little better?''

As his daughter could attest, once having made up his mind, his lordship was loath to change it. Still, he did not like to cross his bride-to-be. ''But I'd hoped to settle the thing before our wedding,'' he protested.

''Which brings us 'round to another matter I wished to broach, m'dear. Only''—she wrinkled her small retroussé nose—''it would not have occurred to me to tackle the thing so early in the morning. But never mind that now. What I wished to ask is whether we might postpone our wedding for a few days.''

''Postpone the wedding! Whatever for?''

''Why, to attend the Lower Wallop Steeplechase, of course. You're dying to go, Devenham. Admit it. And as for me, I'd like to see it above all things.''

''You would?'' He brightened considerably. ''Why, I had no idea that sort of thing appealed to you, m'dear.'' This was all too true. His lordship, on further acquaintance with his bride-to-be, had begun to suspect that they had almost nothing in common outside the bedchamber.

''Well, in the ordinary way of things, racing doesn't appeal to me all that much,'' Mrs. Alden admitted candidly. ''But Plumb is riding in this one, you see. And he's most anxious that I attend.''

''Well, I don't mind saying I'd like to be there. Wouldn't have picked the date we did to marry on if I'd known that they planned to run it then. Thing is, there's never been a steeplechase to match it in these parts. The usual thing is made up of local coves out for a day's sport. But the best horses and riders from all over England will be coming for this one.''

''Then let's go!''

''But what about our guests?'' Devenham shifted in the wing chair uneasily. ''Can't just invite a houseful of people to see us married and then say we've changed our minds about the thing.''

''Whyever not? Most of them plan to stay on for the race, anyhow. And the others will be more than happy to enjoy the country air for a few days longer. Not to mention,'' she added cynically, ''free room and board.''

''By George, then we'll do it!'' His lordship's eyes had brightened considerably. If he had been aware of the change in his expression, he would have attributed it to anticipation of the race. He would never, not in a million years, admit, even to himself, that he was also feeling some relief at this nuptial reprieve.

''Splendid. But now I must admit to some ulterior motives. I am hoping that in these next few days Plumb will succeed in sweeping Cassandra off her feet. And if that happens, I think I know you well enough to believe you won't throw a rub in your daughter's way.

''Still, if the prospect of that romance does not please you, let me throw you a small bone. As you say, people will come from everywhere to see the race. Young gentlemen, especially, will be there in large numbers. And when they see the new, attractive Cassandra, well, it will amaze me if she does not have her pick of beaux.''

''You think so?'' His lordship looked a bit more skeptical than was proper.

''I am sure of it. Oh, Devenham, you are so good to postpone the *Gazette* announcement.'' And before he could voice the protest that was forming, she added, stretching lazily, ''I know just how I can make it up to you.''

''By Jove, I'll wager on it!'' His lordship came quite close to bounding from his chair. Displacing the half-empty chocolate cup, he sat beside his intended on the bed and kissed her hand romantically.

"Instead of two weeks in France, we'll stay two months!"

"Oh, but I say—" Her hand plummeted from his nerveless fingers.

"Just think of it. The two of us. Alone in that romantic country."

His lordship was thinking of it. "Two m-months?" His voice quivered with emotion. "But really, Gwen, m'dear, mustn't stay *that* long."

"Oh, nonsense. There's no need to be back in London till the Little Season."

"In *London*, did you say?" His voice rose half an octave.

"Why, yes, of course. I did mention Lady Buxton's ball, did I not? Surely I must have done, since she's giving it particularly for us. It's high time you came out of your shell, Devenham, and went into society more. And I plan to see to it that you do. Your days as a fusty old bachelor are numbered," she purred. "It's more than time that you took out a new lease on life."

"If you say so, m'dear," Devenham just managed to say.

But there was a notable lack of enthusiasm in his lordship's tone and a decidedly glassy look in his eyes.

Chapter Fourteen

Jeremy Gifford of Bow Street sat gazing around him at the spacious entrance hall, trying not to be overawed by so much grandeur. The starchy butler had almost refused to admit him. It had obviously been on the tip of the man's tongue to direct Jeremy to the servants' entrance. Then, when the Runner had insisted on an audience with Lord Devenham, the butler had derived considerable satisfaction from informing the cit that his lordship was not at home. Nor had he been at all forthcoming about when his lordship was expected back.

But the words *Bow Street* had proved as magical as *Open Sesame*. Once they were uttered, some of the starch evaporated and a rather flustered Parker had elected to see if her ladyship might be available. And he had permitted Jeremy to step inside the portals. But only barely, as if still unconvinced just which side of the law this pugilistic-looking person might be on.

Lady Cassandra was just emerging from her bedchamber

when the somewhat breathless butler came looking for her. She was relieved to see him, for his presence enabled her to ignore Charles, who was coming out of Lord Severn's doorway. Still, she could not quite restrain herself from covertly watching him. And when Parker uttered the words "Bow Street," she saw the valet freeze.

His back was to Cassandra as she made the butler repeat the information that a Bow Street Runner was indeed ensconced in the entrance hall and was desirous of an interview. But she could hardly fail to note the rigid tension in the man or doubt that he was frankly listening. As she preceded Parker toward the staircase, she glanced over her shoulder for a final look. The valet was hurrying toward the servants' stairs.

Meanwhile, Jeremy Gifford perched uncomfortably on the stiff wooden chair where Parker had placed him. His eyes scanned the hall, taking in the curving staircase, the suits of armor, the gilded mirrors, the twin bronzed statuary that held the enormous candelabra aloft. The Runner's mind had no tendency toward envy. It did not dwell on what it might be like to live amidst such opulence. Instead he thought of what a thieves' paradise the hall was. When Lady Cassandra approached him, Mr. Gifford rose respectfully to his feet and stated his business.

No, she informed him with a surge of relief, there was no Captain Danforth staying at Devenham Hall. Indeed, she knew of no such person. Why on earth did Bow Street think he might be among her guests?

Mr. Gifford answered her question with his own. "Is Lord Severn staying at the hall, m'lady?"

"Yes, my cousin is here. Why do you ask? Don't tell me George has run afoul of the law. I won't believe it."

"Oh, no, m'lady," he reassured her hastily. "Nothing like that. It's just that his lordship is a particular friend of the captain's and might know something of his whereabouts. If I could just have a word with Lord Severn."

"At this hour of the morning? He wouldn't thank you for it. My cousin seldom rises before noon. Besides, Lord Severn has a great many friends and can hardly be expected

to account for— Oh, my goodness! I just remembered—"
She broke off, as Mr. Gifford brightened.

"Yes, m'lady?"

"Is this Captain Danforth you mentioned a bruising rider?"

"A nonesuch, so I'm told. Indeed before his, uh, brush with the law, he was expected to win the Lower Wallop Steeplechase. That fact, along with Lord Severn's presence, made it seem quite likely he could be here."

"Well, he isn't. But there's no need to trouble Lord Severn, for now I collect I did hear my cousin tell someone that his friend had gone to France. Not having ever heard of the gentleman before, I fear I paid little heed to the conversation and so it slipped my mind. But there, now you have it. Your quarry is in France. I'm afraid you've had a wasted trip." Her tone was dismissive. She looked pointedly at the door, and Parker, who had been hovering at a discreet distance, sprang to open it.

Mr. Gifford, however, was reluctant to abandon his position. Gaining entrance had been too difficult to allow himself to be expelled so soon. "Begging your pardon, m'lady, but the fact of the matter is, we got a tip that the captain was here at Devenham."

"Who on earth told you such a taradiddle?" she asked.

"The tip was anonymous, your ladyship."

Cassandra began a derisive snort. She tried, with dubious success, to convert it into a cough. "Well," she remarked as soon as she'd recovered, "I am amazed that the law pays any attention to that sort of thing. If an informant won't even reveal his identity, he's not to be trusted, I should think. And it certainly seems a waste of public funds to send an officer all this distance on the basis of mere rumor."

"Oh, you'd be surprised, m'lady, just how often these tips pay off."

"Well, then I suppose you have to play the odds, as the racing world would say. But I fear that in this case you've lost your wager."

"It would seem that way. But the cove who wrote also said that the captain's horse was here."

"Here? In our stables?"

"Yes, m'lady."

"But that's ridiculous. We are not a shelter for stray animals. Have you tried Tattersall's or Tilbury's in London?"

"Naturally, m'lady."

"Well, then, perhaps the animal might be in one of the posting houses in the area. The only cattle here belong to us or to our guests."

"You won't mind, then, if I have a look?"

"Why on earth should you?" Lady Cassandra was at her haughtiest. "I have just told you we have no animals here that are unaccounted for."

"But, begging your ladyship's pardon, isn't it just possible that one of your guests—your cousin, perhaps—could be in possession of the horse?"

"Not my cousin." She spoke emphatically. "For I heard him tell the same inquirer who asked after Captain Danforth that he knew nothing of the horse. He assumed that the captain had taken the animal to France with him, which certainly sounds a lot more likely than having the horse rusticate here, for heaven's sake. The idea's preposterous."

"Not quite so preposterous, m'lady, when you consider the proximity of Devenham Hall to Lower Wallop. So might I just have a look around to satisfy my superiors back in Bow Street? They'd be hard put to understand my coming all this way without so much as a peep inside your stables."

Cassandra made a snap decision. "Very well, then. I'll take you there myself."

Her brain was in a whirl as she guided the Runner to the stables. She barely acknowledged his polite comments on the beauty of his surroundings and the fineness of the day. What she was thinking was absurd, of course. Quite unthinkable, in fact. But still . . .

"You've seen this Captain, er, Danforth's horse before?" she asked abruptly.

"No, m'lady. But I've got a good description. It's a distinctive animal."

In the stable yard, while Cassandra spoke to the head groom, the Runner tried to hide his reaction as he stared at the mammoth, solidly constructed stone building with its decorative cupola. He'd been impervious to the magnificence of the hall. The grandeur of the stables upset him, though. Scarcely anyone he knew was as well housed as these beasts were.

Inside, he went systematically down the stalls, staring at each horse in turn and looking expectantly at the groom when they came to any empty niche. "That's for Lord Morice's bay," the groom would explain. "He's ridden to the village." Or: "this particular stall ain't occupied at the present."

As they drew nearer to the stall where Trafalgar was kept, Cassandra held her breath and tried to look distinterested. Since the Runner did not glance her way, her success or failure was not called into question. She barely managed, though, to stifle a gasp of surprise when a dappled mare, identified by the groom as her latest acquisition, looked up from munching hay to watch the watchers. Now more puzzled than ever, Cassandra approached each remaining stall with trepidation. But at the end of their round, all animals and empty stalls had been accounted for.

"You haven't had a white stallion here recently, have you?" Mr. Gifford asked the groom.

"Why, yes. You saw the one in the fourth stall yourself."

"No, I mean all white. That one had a blaze and some other markings."

"Oh, no. We've had no all-white stallion." The horseman's face was sincere and open. He did, however, avoid looking at Lady Cassandra.

"Or seen one in the neighborhood?"

"Not that I recall."

"Very well, then. I thank you kindly for your time."

The Runner appeared quite satisfied as he took a courteous leave of Lady Cassandra, apologizing for the intrusion.

"I quite understand that you have your duty to perform." She was all graciousness on the surface.

But as soon as Mr. Gifford had disappeared down the drive in his hired gig, Cassandra raced back into the house and up the stairs. The "knock" on Viscount Severn's door came closer to a "whack." Cassandra found it beneficial to suck her knuckles as a muffled voice inside was heard to croak, "Come in."

"Where's Godfrey?" she demanded.

"How the deuce should I know?" Between his nightcap and the sheet, George's eyes opened a tiny crack. "Still in bed if he has any sense."

"No, he isn't. He was up ages ago. Has he come back?"

"Well, you seem to know a lot more about his whereabouts than I do" was the testy answer.

Cassandra strode to the dressing room and peered inside. It was empty. The narrow bed was neatly made, though not, she'd bet a monkey, by Godfrey's hand. "Well, when he comes back, *if* he comes back, tell him I wish to see him. And I'd like a word with you as well, George, after you've revived yourself with a cup of tea." As she closed the door behind her, Cassandra noted with satisfaction that her cousin was sitting up. The expression on his face was apprehensive.

Trusting neither to chance nor to George, Cassandra left her own chamber door wide open. She positioned a chair to command a good view of the hall. It was no sign of her preoccupation that she frequently botched the sampler she was working on. Cassandra's tambouring had been the despair of her time at the Academy for Young Ladies. What was amazing was her persistence. For she kept at the task for three-quarters of an hour, until at last she spied the valet's head rising slowly above the threshold of the servants' stairs.

"Godfrey! I'd like a word with you."

"He started like a guilty thing surprised," Cassandra

thought, rather proud of dredging up such an appropriate quotation.

"With me, m'lady?" The valet's expression had instantly grown bland, his eyes innocent.

"Yes, Godfrey, with you." She stood by her door and, with a commanding gesture, ushered him inside, then closed it firmly behind him.

"Do take a seat, Captain Danforth," she said.

Chapter Fifteen

*C*aptain Charles Danforth took Lady Cassandra's offer one step further and stretched out full-length on a crocodile-legged settee. "At least I'm glad to see," she observed as she pulled up a stool opposite him, "that you are not going to waste time by denying who you are." If the truth were told, she was nettled by his nonchalance. She had expected a great deal more in the way of a reaction.

"Would it do any good to try to deny it? I was toying with the notion of pretending to be Captain Danforth's illegitimate brother, often mistaken for him. But something told me it wouldn't wash."

"No, it would not. And I don't think it's in your interest just now to remind me of the Banbury tales you've already spun—the father whose burning ambition is for you to become a butler, for instance. Of all the . . ." she sputtered as words failed her and left her with only an indignant glare to express her sentiments.

"Tales? I prefer to call my stories fables. And as with all good fables, mine contained a nugget of truth."

" 'Truth,' Captain Danforth? I cannot believe that truth and you are often in harness."

"Oh, I say." The captain did, indeed, look offended now. "That's rather unfair, Cassandra. You can't possibly know what—"

"*Lady* Cassandra," she interrupted with frosty hauteur. "And you are right, sir. I could not possibly know all your reasons for persuading my cousin to abuse our hospitality by harboring a criminal."

The captain winced at the stinging epithet. He reached into the recesses of his coat and pulled out a large cigar.

"You surely do not intend to smoke! What will my maid think?"

"Either that you've taken up the vile habit yourself or that a man's been in your bedchamber," he answered between rapid puffs as he lighted up.

"Captain Danforth, I'm trying to discuss a serious matter."

"*Lady* Cassandra, I'm well aware of the gravity of my situation."

"I wonder if you truly are. But to proceed. I do not know, nor do I care to speculate, why you are on the run from the law. But I've a very good notion of why you've chosen this for your hideout."

"Because George is here?" he offered helpfully.

"No! Oh, of course, if George weren't here you wouldn't have come as his valet—oh, do quit muddying the waters, Captain Danforth. I'm trying to tell you that I know you're hiding here so you can race at Lower Wallop. Am I not right?" He nodded, and she continued. "And when you saw Mr. Gifford of Bow Street, you ran to the stables and spirited Trafalgar away."

"Wrong." He blew a smoke ring and watched its ascension to the ceiling. "I ran to the stables and bribed the grooms not to mention that they'd seen Trafalgar. I had already taken the precaution of removing my horse when it occurred to me that Mr. Davies might try to eliminate me from the competition.''

"Mr. Davies? The Runner did say that someone had given them a tip that you were here, but surely Mr. Davies would not do such a thing? At least not for the reason you imply: to keep you out of the race in order to give himself a better chance. Why, that would be ungentlemanly and unsportsmanlike.''

"Oh, it would be both of those things, certainly. Not even to mention underhanded and knavish.''

"Of course, if Mr. Davies were the one who tipped off Bow Street,'' she mused, "in all fairness we should not overlook the fact that you *are* a wanted criminal.''

"I say, would you mind substituting the word *fugitive* occasionally for *criminal*? Sounds rather less villainous, don't you think?''

"So if Mr. Davies did report you, perhaps he was motivated by civic responsibility.''

"And perhaps pigs fly.''

"Well, enough of Mr. Davies. It's not his conduct that's at issue here, it's yours. What we need to talk about is what action I should take.''

"About to become civically responsible, too, are you?''

"Not unless given no other choice. Here, sir, is what I propose to do.''

As Lady Cassandra began to outline her plan, Charles Danforth lost the last shred of his studied nonchalance. He forgot to smoke. His cigar went out. His chin dropped. His eyes glazed over. And when Cassandra had concluded her rehearsed speech and looked at him expectantly, no words came. "Well?'' she prodded.

Finally he found his tongue. "No! No, by gad! It's blackmail!'' he exploded. "I'll have no part in such a shatter-brained, knuckle-headed, sap-skulled scheme!''

"Oh, really?'' She smiled archly. "Well, then, Captain Danforth, enjoy your stay in France.''

He glared at her, barely suppressing the urge to strangle her; while at the same time he managed to marvel that he had actually feared he was falling in love with this—this

. . . But then, hadn't Sisera been kindly disposed toward Jael just before she pounded the tent peg into his temple?

"No need to work your shabby tricks on me." He walked across the room and ground the end of his cigar viciously, and unnecessarily, into a china basin on the washstand. "It don't matter how I feel about your insane idea." He chose the lion's-head couch this time but sat upright on it. "You need George's support more than you need mine. And he won't stand still for it."

"Oh, yes, he will." Cassandra looked quite sure of herself. "It's obvious that no sacrifice is too great for George where your friendship is concerned. The fact he made do without Chesney is testimony to the lengths he's prepared to go to. Aiding me won't be an odious circumstance compared to that. Shall we ask him?"

"Yes, let's do just that." He rose to his feet. "And prepare yourself for a bit of a shock. I think you'll find George adamant. He was, as you say, willing to do just about anything for me. But what you propose concerns the family honor. Oh, he'll throw me to the wolves, all right. And, by Jupiter, I won't blame him."

Now it was Cassandra's turn to glare. Like Charles, she was beginning to have second thoughts about the state of her emotions. Her first wave of relief over not being half in love with a member of the servant class had been short-lived. Now she had begun to wonder if she did not prefer the subservient Godfrey to the arrogant Captain Danforth.

"Let me go in first to see if he's decent," he commanded as they reached her cousin's door. "George ain't likely to be as insensitive to the proprieties as you are."

While he opened the door and peered inside, Cassandra was considering the consequences of kicking an ex–cavalry captain's shins. The only thing that saved him was an abrupt change of manner. He stepped back deferentially. "Lady Cassandra wishes a word, your lordship." He ushered her inside.

She managed to bite back a snide comment as she saw the reason for prolonging his charade. Mr. Davies's valet was putting the final touches to George's cravat. It took a few seconds of frantic pantomime behind Standen's back before enlightenment broke through. "Uh, that will do now, thank you." George dismissed the valet. As the door closed behind the servant, he rose to his feet and faced the two interlopers with alarm.

"I think you'd best sit back down, old fellow." Charles got straight to the point. "Your cousin has gone stark, raving mad and now intends to involve us in her lunacy. The club she's holding over our heads is that she plans to tell Bow Street to come and get me if we don't do exactly as she says."

"Oh, I say!" George was looking at his cousin with decided disapproval. "Wouldn't't've thought that of you, Cassie."

"Oh, don't pay any attention to his high flights, George. It won't come to that. What I'm asking of you is a very small thing, really."

Captain Danforth's snort was a masterpiece of derision, intended to discourage a mere female from ever trying to match its timbre. "A small thing, really," he mimicked. "I just want you to know, George, that I'll think no less of you when you tell her to write Bow Street and be damned."

"I suggest that you let me talk to my cousin alone." Lady Cassandra's tone and frown were both dismissive.

But all traces of Godfrey had gone. Captain Danforth flung himself on his friend's bed and lounged against the pillows with his arms behind his head. "I wouldn't miss this for the world. Go on and tell him what you have in mind."

"George, I intend to ride in the Lower Wallop Steeplechase. I've been thinking of it for ages, ever since I learned how much money was involved. It's a perfect way out of the coil I'm in, you see. My winnings will make it possible for me to set up a household independently without Papa's approval. The problem was, I didn't know how to go about the thing. But with you to help me, there'll be nothing to it."

George's eyes threatened to pop from his head. He felt

a sudden need for solid support and collapsed in a chair, while Cassandra stood over him. "Charlie's right. You have gone queer in the attic."

"Don't be absurd, George. It's a reasonable course of action when you stop to think on it."

"Reasonable!" Her cousin choked. Then, just as suddenly, he simmered down. "Well, I *am* thinking on it and there's no use my getting into such a taking over your addlepated scheme, for they ain't about to let a woman ride in the steeplechase, and that's that."

"Do you think I'm not aware of their prejudice? I don't intend to ride as a woman. And that, George, is where you come in."

The viscount's groan was piteous.

"As I understand it, the plan that you and he"—she gestured toward the bed without deigning to look that way—"have concocted is that you're going to enter Trafalgar in the race with you as the rider, then at the last minute you'll make a switch. Am I not right?" Her cousin nodded. "Well, all I'm asking is that you enter Pegasus as well."

"And am I supposed to be riding two horses in the race?"

Charles Danforth sniggered at the viscount's sarcasm.

"No, of course not. Eustace will be riding Pegasus."

"Eustace! My little brother! How the devil can he? He's at Harrow. Besides, the lad's no better a rider than I am. Worse, in fact."

"Worse? Oh, come now, George. That's hardly possible," said Charles.

Cassandra continued to ignore all remarks coming from the bed. But she did not bother to stifle her impatience with her cousin's thickheadedness. "I'm not the least concerned with Eustace's riding skill, for heaven's sake. He won't be riding Pegasus. I will. Pretending to be Eustace."

"You can't be serious, Cassandra. You're bamming me. Bound to be."

"Nothing of the sort. The plan is perfectly reasonable. Eustace and I are about the same height and coloring. In fact, I should say there's a strong family resemblance. And dressed like the other riders, with my cap pulled down to shield my face, I would look like everybody else."

"If you do, I plan to find another field." This comment came from the direction of the bed.

"You see, George, I plan to take my cue from the criminal here and keep out of sight until the horses line up for the race. And at that point the other riders should have their minds on more pressing matters than my identity. Really, there's no reason it should not work."

Offhand, George was sure that there must be at least a thousand. He uttered the first one that came into his head. "Have you thought that it would be just like Eustace to slip away from school and come to the race?"

"Well, yes, that did occur to me," Cassandra replied. "I'll simply have to write and take him into my confidence. I think he'll consider the whole thing a famous lark and not dream of throwing a rub in my way. He's not henhearted like you, George."

"Oh, you won't make your cousin come around by taunting him, Cassandra," Charles told her. "George is above that kind of thing."

"I was not taunting him! Oh, very well, then, perhaps I was. Pray forgive me, George. Besides, here's an argument that should carry much more weight. Just let me point out, cousin, that your criminal friend's freedom is not the only thing riding on your cooperation. Your freedom is also at stake. Papa just may bully us into a marriage if I can't forestall him by becoming independent."

"Now I call that low" was Captain Danforth's observation.

George, however, was not as moved by this last argument as the others had expected him to be. "Oh, I don't doubt for a minute your papa will get his way on that score," he said with an unflattering sigh. "The thing is, what you suggest ain't going to stop him. Oh, your little scheme may give Charlie here a reprieve, all right. But it ain't going to make a tuppence worth of difference where our marriage is concerned. For not to put too fine a point on it, the notion that you could win is moonshine."

Cassandra bristled.

Charles gave a hoot of laughter. "I wondered just which one of us would have to say it. Thank you, Severn."

Cassandra, ready to blister George, redirected her fire. "It's been perfectly obvious all along, Captain Danforth, why you do not wish me to enter the steeplechase. You know that Pegasus can beat your Trafalgar."

"Don't be daft."

"Daft? What's daft about an assertion that's already been put to the test?"

He was no longer lounging but sitting upright. " 'Put to the test'? What the devil to you mean?" Suddenly his eyes widened and he started to laugh, collapsing back weakly against the pillows. "Don't tell me you got this maggoty notion into your head because old Godfrey let your horse outrun his. Oh, dear lord! That's too ridiculous by half!"

Cassandra did not share Captain Danforth's sense of humor. She watched him coldly until his mirth subsided. "You *let* me win, you say?"

"Naturally. What else could a poor valet do?"

Cassandra snorted. Deliberately. With malice aforethought. "That, Captain Danforth, is the same old threadbare excuse given by every man who has ever been bested by a woman."

Charles sat up once more. His eyes were narrowed. "You have no reason to doubt my word, Cassandra."

Her eyebrows rose significantly.

"Oh, very well, then, let me amend that. What I mean is, you would be well advised to accept what I say as the gospel. I did let you win that day. Your Pegasus could not outrun Trafalgar in a million years."

"You had better listen, Cassandra," George chimed in. "For when it comes to this sort of thing, no one's more knowing than Charlie here. Oh, I say!" His eyes gleamed with the light of inspiration. "Why don't you simply put your blunt on Trafalgar to win? Bound to make a bundle. And that's what this is really all about, isn't it?"

Cassandra did not bother to reply. Perhaps it was because she didn't know what to say. Perhaps money had originally been the moving force in her decision to enter the steeplechase, but it now was being supplanted by a more compelling need.

"Do I understand you to be saying, Captain, that you have the better horse?" she asked.

"Undoubtedly."

"I'm not convinced of that. Neither, I collect, are you. Why else would you be so determined to keep me from the field? I think you're afraid to race me, Captain Danforth."

"Pay no attention, Charlie," George told him. "Know what I'm thinking? That it's all a hum, anyhow. Have known Cassie since we were both in leading strings and she ain't the kind to throw a fellow to the wolves just to get her way. Be honest, Cassie. Could you live with your conscience if you were the cause of Charlie here rotting in Newgate?"

"My conscience would have nothing to say in the matter. I did not cause Captain Danforth to break the law. I hold him responsible for his own fate."

"Oh, but, I say, you don't even know—"

"Don't bother, George. You're wasting your time trying to appeal to your cousin's tender nature. And wasting your chivalry trying to keep her from making a cake of herself. As long as Lady Cassandra realizes what she's letting herself in for if she enters the steeplechase—including eating Trafalgar's dust at the finish line—well, I say let's stop trying to throw a rub in her way."

"That's very handsome of you." Cassandra's looks, somehow, belied her statement. "And I do know what I'm in for, a lot better than you do, obviously. For you'll eat your words before I eat your dust. But how about you, George? Do you also agree?"

"No. I don't like it one little bit." The viscount's jaw was set stubbornly.

"Oh, come on, George. Her mind's made up. Might as well give in gracefully." Charles had done an about-face. Instead of being horrified at the prospect of Cassandra's racing, he now seemed to find the idea amusing. "Where's your sporting blood, old man?"

"Running cold in my veins right now," the viscount retorted. "But I can tell you where it's going to be. Spilled all down the front of my shirt, most likely! For when my Uncle Devenham discovers I've aided and abetted his only daughter to enter a gentlemen's steeplechase . . . Well, he's bound to draw my claret, no mistake."

Chapter Sixteen

Plumb Davies was itching to learn the results of Mr.
Jeremy Gifford's visit. He introduced the subject as the
company, for the most part, settled in the drawing room
for an evening of whist. He and Cassandra were pitted
against Lord Devenham and Mrs. Alden. The latter team
was not a happy partnership since his lordship was highly
competitive and Mrs. Alden's mind tended to wander from
the play. Mr. Davies's casual remark could have been seen
as an attempt to ease the tension caused by Devenham's
reaction to his partner's unfortunate choice of card.

"I understand there was a Bow Street Runner here today." Most of his attention seemed to be on the cards that
he was shuffling.

"Eh, what?" His lordship jerked his mind off the mis-
played queen of diamonds. "What's that you say? A Runner here at the hall? First I've heard of it."

"Indeed? Then perhaps you know something of the matter, Lady Cassandra?"

"Well, yes. I did talk to the man."

"Why the devil didn't you tell me so, miss?" Lord Devenham was glad to find a more appropriate target than his fiancée for his annoyance.

"It slipped my mind. I'm sorry, Papa. It was much ado about nothing, anyhow. He was looking for a Captain Danforth. Seems he's a friend of George's and the Runner thought he might be among the company here."

"Well, I must say that George has some rackety friends. Running from the law! Shameful! Danforth, did you say? Any relation to the Gloucester Danforths?"

"He's Lord Meredith's son, I understand," Davies replied.

"Oh, yes. It comes back to me now. Oldest boy died. The younger was something of a scapegrace."

"Oh, I wouldn't call Charlie a scapegrace, Devenham." Mrs. Alden was quick to spring to the captain's defense. "His military career was quite distinguished. Actually, he was something of a hero, wasn't he, Plumb?"

"So I've been given to understand. But you're right in a way, m'lord. The Honorable Charles was always a bit on the wild side. Rather made for the army, actually. It's not easy to imagine him settling down."

"Really now, that's hardly fair." Mrs. Alden's usual amiability seemed a trifle frayed. The queen of diamonds had a lot to answer for. "You must remember, Plumb, that Charlie was not bred to be the heir. You must allow him some time to make adjustments."

His lordship frowned. "Know this fugitive from the law well, do you?"

"Not to say 'well.' But, yes, we are acquainted."

"You'll have to resign yourself, Lord Devenham"—Mr. Davis smiled as he dealt the cards—"to the fact that there's no handsome man between eighteen and eighty that Gwenny here doesn't know."

"What I'm curious about, Mr. Davies, is just how you happened to know the Runner was here." Cassandra hoped that her question would appear to be a tactful change of subject and not an accusation.

"Ah, now you have caught me out." Cassandra stared in amazement. Was he actually going to admit that he'd sent the note to Bow Street? "The terrible truth is, dear lady, that when I saw you stroll toward the stables with another man . . . Well, I became an instant victim of the green-eyed monster, in spite of the fact that even at a distance the fellow did seem to be a cit. Still, one could not be sure. He might have been a rival. So I made inquiries of your butler."

"Oh" was the only comment Cassandra trusted herself to make after such a taradiddle.

"Why the devil did the chap want to see the stables?" His lordship looked up from frowning at his hand. "Did he expect to find Danforth hiding there?"

"No, sir. He was looking for the captain's horse."

"His horse! If the fellow's not here, then why the devil would his horse be?"

"The race, Lord Devenham," Mr. Davies replied. "Till Captain Danforth was forced to take to his heels, he was one of the top contenders for the Lower Wallop crown."

"You're wrong, Plumb." Mrs. Alden seemed to have forgotten all of those precepts she'd lectured on to Cassandra. Pleasing the other sex had become a low priority. "Charlie was *the* top contender. The odds-on favorite."

"I would not go quite that far, Gwennie dear." Mr. Davies's smile was forced. "I have my admirers, too, you know."

"Are we going to play or ain't we?" his lordship inquired grumpily. "Start us off, Gwendolen. And do try to remember what's been played this time. We can't let these two get the better of us."

"I shall do my best." Mrs. Alden sighed. "But really, Devenham, does it matter? You seem to forget that whist is, after all, only a game."

"Har-harrumph!" was the only comment his lordship could safely allow himself to make.

"Your suspicions are probably correct," Lady Cassandra informed Captain Danforth as they met by arrangement early the next morning. They were riding sedately side by side, as if neither wished to call attention to their new status as racing archrivals. Each covertly assessed the points of the other's mount, however, with even more interest in horseflesh than they'd previously shown. "It was Mr. Davies who reported you to the authorities, I'm all but certain. At least he seemed to be the only one of the guests aware that we'd been paid a visit by Bow Street."

"That issue was never in doubt."

"You can't be positive. He didn't actually admit it. In fact, he said his interest was in me and not my visitor."

"Fustian."

"Thank you very much. I, myself, did not find that quite so impossible."

"No need to get on your high ropes. I was not implying that you aren't worth the interest. It's simply that I know Davies a bit too well. The man's a wily scoundrel."

"Well, I won't argue that." They rode in silence up the hill where she'd watched Godfrey through the spyglass. After a struggle, Cassandra finally managed to say, "I must admit it's handsome of you, Captain Danforth, to show me the steeplechase paces. After all, we are competitors."

Charles sighed. "No, it isn't handsome at all. Frankly, Cassandra, what I'm hoping is that once you realize what's involved, you'll drop this lunatic notion. Believe me, a steeplechase is no sort of race for a woman. It's the most dangerous form of sport."

"I'm well aware of that, Captain." Her jaw was set in a stubborn line. "And if you'd rather not add to my advantage, it's quite understandable. I shall certainly not hold it against you."

Captain Danforth swore—at length, fluently, and, almost, silently. "Come along, then." He concluded his tirade by giving Trafalgar a kick. "Be it on your own conscience when you break your beautiful, stiff neck."

Cassandra was momentarily diverted. She was not accustomed to having the word *beautiful* applied to herself. And even if it only described an insignificant part of her anatomy in an insulting sort of way, it did have a nice ring to it.

But she soon forgot all else in the serious business of water jumps and hedgerows. She gave her rival credit. He did seem intent on letting her know exactly what she was up against. "You won't be riding to hounds, you realize" was the way he concluded his demonstration.

"Of course, I know that." Her scornful tone served as much to dampen down her faint misgivings as to put him in his place. "Have you ridden in many of these events?" she asked as they slowed their horses to a walk to cool them down.

"Quite a few."

"And have you won any?"

He gave her a level look. "I've won them all."

"Oh, what a pity. Then you've had no practice in being a good loser."

He laughed, but quickly sobered. "I really wish I could convince you to drop this plan, Cassandra. And not for the reason you insist on attributing to me."

She ignored the obvious concern in his eyes. This was not the time to grow fainthearted, or to think of how attractive he was when he looked so serious, or to dwell on the fact that riding with this man over the green countryside with the wind in her face and the sun beaming overhead just might possibly be the most pleasant thing she'd done in her entire life. To nip this sort of musing in the bud, she asked, "Have you ever ridden the course at Lower Wallop?"

"No."

"You do realize that that places you at a real disadvantage?"

"Yes. And the same goes for you."

"But I intend to go over it when I get there. Oh, not as Cousin Eustace. I'm counting heavily on the excitement of race time to make that disguise effective. I fear it would not hold up under ordinary conditions when I might be singled out for scrutiny."

"Well, thank God you realize you'll make a damned unconvincing boy."

Again, she chose to ignore his contribution to the exchange. "But no one will think anything of it if I—accompanied by my groom, naturally—ride over the course, just to observe what the racers will be up against the next day. Any female might do the same, might she not?"

"Well, not *any* female, perhaps. But very well, then, I do agree that no one's likely to refine too much on it. Go ahead and take your ride—accompanied by your groom, of course. Never let it be said that Lady Cassandra Devenham would behave improperly."

"Such sarcasm hardly becomes a man who recently, in my hearing, was called a scapegrace." They paused to let their horses now drink from a brook they'd gone leaping over a bit before.

"Scapegrace? Well, I've been called worse in my time. But I'm not sure I can live up to that description. 'Here-and-thereian' is about as far as my villainy can stretch. Mr. Davies's description, I suppose?"

"No, Papa's."

"Oh."

"But don't be downcast. Mrs. Alden immediately sprang to your defense. You would have found no fault with her advocacy."

"From your tone, I take it you did. Find fault, I mean."

"Well, I must confess it does worry me a bit that my father's bride is on such intimate terms with a here-and-thereian. Especially now that I must discard the notion that your father was an old family retainer and you and she shared a nursery together."

He chuckled, and she frowned. "I really don't find Mrs. Alden's Banbury tale as amusing as you seem to." They guided their horses out of the stream. "Nor would my father be amused if he should discover your odd relationship."

"You're certain that your concern is all for your father?"

"Naturally. You surely don't think I could be concerned for Mrs. Alden?"

"No, I didn't have her in mind." He gazed at Cassandra thoughtfully, and she reddened a bit.

"We seem to have strayed entirely from the subject," she rallied. "What I was going to say was that once I've studied the steeplechase course at Lower Wallop, I'll be happy to share the information with you. Unless, of course, you intend to explore it yourself."

"That would be imprudent, I'm afraid."

"You think the law will be on the lookout for you?"

"Undoubtedly. Our friend Plumb will see to that."

"Well, I hope you're mistaken. I don't like Mr. Davies above half, but I can't believe he has no more principle than to knock a rival out of the race in such a fashion." Her indignation might have seemed hypocritical except for the fact that they both knew now she could never have informed on the captain herself.

"Believe it. And whatever you do, don't let him learn you plan to race. He's not above nobbling Pegasus, you know."

"He wouldn't!" She gasped.

"If he had half the opinion of your chances that you have, he'd do it in a minute. Of course," he said with a grin, "that ain't too likely. Plumb's a devilish fine odds maker and not likely to rate you high."

"Don't push me, Captain," she retorted, "or I may renege on my promise to share the course topography."

"Wouldn't blame you. You need all the advantage you can get. Oh, this is as far as I go." He pulled on Trafalgar's rein, and Cassandra obligingly stopped beside him.

"You must have Trafalgar hidden on Ned Green's farm," she remarked shrewdly. "But as for what you were implying, I wouldn't dream of taking advantage of your ignorance of the racecourse. Nothing's going to dilute my satisfaction in beating you. So, how can we arrange a meeting in Lower Wallop? You surely don't plan to go with George as Godfrey?"

"No. Too risky by half. Every racing cove in England knows me," was the immodest, though accurate, answer. "Not that they'd give me away on purpose. But I'd likely keep cropping up in conversations and Runners have big ears.''

"Then how shall I get the information to you?''

"Oh, I'll manage to send you word.''

"Very well, then.''

Cassandra seemed at a loss as to what to say now. She stared at Pegasus's neck and began awkwardly, "Thank you again for your instruction. I was right. You would have made a first-rate groom. Good-bye, Captain Danforth. I suppose I shall see you next at Lower Wallop," she finished formally.

"I shall look forward to it, your ladyship.'' There was a tinge of Godfrey in his tone and bow. "And, oh, your ladyship!'' he called as she nudged Pegasus and cantered off.

"Yes?'' She reined in and turned around.

"May the best man win!''

"Oh, she will, Captain. Never fear, she will!'' With a sudden grin and an airy wave of the hand, Cassandra urged her mount into a showoff burst of speed.

Charles sat gazing after them till horse and rider had disappeared over the hilltop. His face reflected his inner turmoil. Admiration was vying with disgust to be his dominant emotion.

Chapter Seventeen

Cassandra abandoned the idea of sleep. She had tossed and turned all night, excited by (certainly not nervous about) the prospect of the race. In her mind, she had gone over every inch of the terrain that she and George had examined the evening before, and when she finally did fall asleep around two o'clock, it was to dream that she was trying to make it across that appalling wall in the third mile with Pegasus clinging to her back. Now there was far too much commotion outside the inn to permit the few more winks she'd been attempting. Cassandra opened the eyes that she'd been determined to keep shut and crawled out of her curtained bed.

She dressed quickly, then went to lean out of the casement window that overlooked the inn yard. Her first instinct was to check the sky. The sun was rising fair. She breathed a deep sigh of relief. Riding that arduous seven-mile course in the rain and mud—well, that was unthinkable. Under the best of conditions it might still prove too— That was unthinkable also. She pulled her gaze from the heavens to consider the scene below.

In spite of the early hour, the courtyard of the Fighting Cock and the village street that skirted it hummed with excitement. Indeed, there had hardly been a moment all night long when Cassandra had not heard the jingle of harness, the murmur of voices. But now such subdued disturbances were superceded by a cacophony of noise. There was the clatter of hooves, the rumble of wheels, the tramp of feet, and the shout of voices. As the sun's rim appeared, no one made a pretense any longer of toning down any type of racket in deference to sleeping guests. There were more important things than sleep to be considered. The burning question of which special horse out of a field of twenty-four would succeed in galloping from point to point over seven miles of treacherous terrain, outracing and outjumping all of its opponents, was to be settled once and for all that very day.

And from every place imaginable, people converged upon the tiny village of Lower Wallop to turn it into an instant metropolis. They came from every direction, from all walks of life. The city dwellers, the folk from the hamlets, the rich, the poor, the young, the old, male and female, they gathered, reduced to a common denominator of excitement.

Staring down at the throng streaming along the road, already intent on establishing a good vantage point to view a race not scheduled to begin until eleven o'clock, Cassandra felt a sudden rush of fear, like an actor peeping through the curtain before the show begins. Oh, dear. This won't do, she thought, and went in search of George.

It was a testimony to the pervasive excitement that her slugabed cousin was already up and dressed when Cassandra tapped lightly at his door. The reunited Chesney gave her a respectful bow; then, checking his master's sartorial splendor and seeing that it was perfect, he retired.

"You're dressed for the race already." Cassandra looked her cousin up and down, taking in every detail of his scarlet hunting coat, snowy buckskins, shiny black spurred boots. "Oh, George, will I ever manage to look like that?"

"Not in a million years" was the dampening rejoinder. "Really, Cassie, you ought to forget—"

"Did you bring my clothes?" She did not wish to hear the end of his remonstrance.

"Of course." He sighed. "They're hanging in the press there." He nodded at a huge wardrobe that took up a good portion of his bedchamber wall.

"Did Chesney think it odd that you brought along another riding outfit?"

The viscount looked pained. "Chesney realizes the perils of becoming mud-splashed or of having someone's ale jostled all over one's pink coat. I would not dream of coming unprepared. You did bring your own boots, I hope. I don't think mine will fit. Not to say my other clothes will, either. You're bound to look a fright."

This broke some of Cassandra's tension and she laughed. "Never mind, George. No one should notice. At least not until I win."

"Oh, God." George groaned. "Cassandra, you still haven't the slightest idea of what you're in for, have you? Which reminds me"—he walked over to pick up a folded paper from the dressing table—"here's a note from Charlie."

"Oh, then you did give him the description of the course that I sketched out for him?"

"Naturally. I'm beginning to feel like a curst mail coach."

"Where's Charlie staying? Captain Danforth, I mean to say."

"He spent the night in the loft."

"Oh, my goodness! He can't have rested well. That could cost him."

"I wouldn't waste my time worrying about Charlie if I were you." The viscount sounded grim. "I tell you, Cassandra, if you don't break your neck out there during the race, well, your papa's going to do it for you afterward.

Which ain't a circumstance close to what he'll do to me when he finds out I've been an accessory."

She was too busy reading her letter to heed her cousin's prophecy of doom.

"Cassandra," the note began with no proper salutation. In spite of herself, she smiled at his informality. Then she frowned. She had never given him permission to make free with her Christian name. He'd simply begun the practice soon after his unmasking. "I don't think I was half so fidgety on the eve of Waterloo," the note went on, to Cassandra's great relief. If a veteran like Captain Danforth could admit to butterflies, what she was feeling, then, was only natural. The next sentence, though, pulled the rug from under her newfound confidence.

> *I should have tied you in your own attic before I became a party to what you're planning. Please, please, Cassandra, I implore you. Don't race today!*

Why that—that—that epitome of male conceit wasn't at all anxious about his own part in the steeplechase. *She* was the sole cause of his nervousness! If Cassandra felt a moment's glow at his concern for her, it was certainly short-lived. How dare he be so patronizing! She read on.

> *Well, at least now my conscience is made a little easier by this last-ditch attempt to bring you to your senses. (It can never be entirely easy. But it's too late now for the aforementioned rope in the afore-mentioned attic.) But I can well imagine the results of all my pleading. You've flown up into the boughs and are more determined than ever that you're going to race and beat me.*

Again, Cassandra smiled. It even occurred to her to wonder if the captain was being deliberately provoking to give her an outlet for her nerves. No, that was entirely too subtle for a here-and-thereian like Danforth.

145

*But at least let me give you some last-minute point-
ers that I may not have touched upon while we were
practicing. It's the least I can do in exchange for the
expert way you scouted the course for me. So here
goes. And don't sit there telling yourself you know
all this already. It never hurts to review before any
examination.*

1. *A lot of riders beat themselves by getting overeager. So stay cool and let 'em do it.*
2. *Remember, a balking horse generally swerves left.
Watch for it.*
3. *Don't rush your fences. Give Pegasus time. Then
steady him about twenty yards from the jump. He
needs your confidence.*
4. *Keep your eyes open for the best takeoff and landing spots. You've got to plan ahead.*
5. *Above all, remember this. The first six and a half
miles are prelude. It's the last half mile that
counts. So gauge your pace. Be sure Pegasus has
enough steam left to make the finish. And keep
your spurs to yourself till they're really needed.*
6. *And, finally, try and be a gracious loser when you
follow Trafalgar's rump over the finish line.*

> *yrs truly & affcty,*
> *Charlie*

"Of all the conceited, puffed-up, cocks of the walk!"
Words failed her. She wadded the missive and threw it
across the room.

"Really, Cassandra," George chided, "that's most unfair. Charlie's worried sick over you riding this steeplechase. Says he'd just as lief see you take part in a cavalry
charge."

"He'd do better to concern himself with his own wel-
fare." Cassandra walked over to retrieve the letter and
smooth out its creases.

George watched her and shook his head.

* * *

Though free of Cassandra's anxieties, Mrs. Alden was also denied her beauty sleep. At about the same time her future stepdaughter had gone in search of George, there was a brisk tapping on the widow's door. Mr. Davies was faintly surprised when a wide-awake voice called, "Come in." He found Mrs. Alden propped up in bed, drinking tea.

"You amaze me, m'love," Mr. Davies remarked as he crossed the room to kiss her lightly on the cheek, then sat on the edge of the bed. "I had thought I would have to wake you."

"Who could sleep with all this hullabaloo?" She yawned and gestured toward her window, which, like Cassandra's, opened on the yard. "Not you, obviously. Can't believe you're already dressed."

Mr. Davies was wearing the prescribed scarlet. And while his elegance was no match for the perfection of the Viscount Severn, still, he cut a noble figure, which Mrs. Alden was quick to appreciate. "La, Plumb, a gentleman never dresses to better advantage then when he rides. Not even on the dance floor," she observed, helping herself to a Sally Lund.

"Whereas the boudoir is the lady's element," he murmured, bending over for a sticky, prolonged kiss.

"Would you like some tea?" she asked a few moments later as he applied her napkin to his lips.

"No, thank you, m'dear. I'm breakfasting at eight with some of my fellow sportsmen. I just stopped to ask a favor of you."

She eyed him suspiciously. "Might've known. What kind of favor? Nothing I'm apt to regret, I trust."

"No, of course not. And nothing that's going to cause undue exertion on your part. I simply want you to help ensure that Danforth don't race today."

Mrs. Alden's cup met its saucer with a suddenness that almost cracked it. "How on earth could I possibly do a thing like that? Even if I *wanted* to do a thing like that? And, I must say, I don't like the idea at all. Charlie's a dear friend. There are limits to what I'm prepared to do. Even for you, Plumb."

"Are there, my dear?" He ran his fingers lightly down her throat and smiled lazily. "Perhaps you've forgotten what winning this race means to me. To *us*. And Charlie Danforth won't be any the worse for losing. Oh, he may have to cool his heels in France awhile. But the future Lord Meredith won't be up the River Tick for long. His father's bound to bail him out once the old man thinks his heir has learned his lesson. No, my love, I'm the one who needs your sympathy."

Mrs. Alden sighed and then capitulated. "Very well. What is it you wish of me, Plumb?"

"Just make sure the Runner knows that Charlie plans to race. That's all you'll have to do. You can rest assured he'll be there ready to nab Danforth at the starting line."

"I don't like it above half! Me turning informer! What will people say? Charlie's well liked. And there's no use thinking a thing like that won't get about. Even if I ask the Bow Street person not to drag my name into the affair, he's bound to."

"No, no, no, m'dèar." Mr. Davies looked pained. "Would I ask you to do anything as crude as that? Of course you would never betray a friend. Quite unthinkable. Here's what you'll do."

It was George's idea that they take a look at the horses. "Help kill some time for you" was his explanation to Cassandra, but she didn't believe for a moment that the viscount's concern was all for her. "You're worried about Trafalgar, aren't you?"

"As a matter of fact, I am," he admitted. "Davies ain't managed to get Charlie arrested yet," he added gloomily, "so I wouldn't put it past him to have somebody nobble his horse. Just the kind of thing he would do."

They strolled out into the confusion of the inn yard, where special coaches from London were disgorging passengers, where gigs, curricles, landaus, phaetons, and barouches vied for space. Dressed in a cream-colored muslin walking dress topped with a dark green spencer and set off by a matching low-crowned, wide-brimmed hat, Cassandra looked the very soul of propriety as she placed a cream-kid-gloved hand daintily on George's scarlet sleeve. Heads that turned to gaze at the elegant young pair held no notion of the scandalous course the young lady was bent on pursuing.

George had thought to avoid the crowds that thronged the street by taking a field path behind the inn that would lead them to the stables. But the quiet rural landscape they'd strolled through just last evening had been instantly transformed. The path that had then wound through empty fields was now flanked by booths and stalls and carts of all descriptions, whose occupants were hawking wares of every kind. Tumblers and acrobats, nut-brown fortune tellers and horse traders, itinerant musicians and actors—all the varieties of those nomads to be found on the outskirts of every racecourse, fair, and village green were out in force.

Cassandra was diverted enough to wish to pause and watch a swarthy gypsy dressed in bright red spangles swallow flame to the imperilment of a curly jet-black beard, but George pulled her determinedly through the throng until they came upon a scantily dressed female with castanets doing an exotic dance, and it was Cassandra's turn to remind him of their mission.

They were by no means the only temporary residents of Lower Wallop who had decided to take one last look at the horseflesh who would make or break their fortunes this fateful day. Swells and cits jostled and elbowed one another for a better look at their favorites, while the wary among them kept a weather eye out for the inevitable pickpockets plying their trade among the crowd.

Cassandra and George had no problem making their way to Pegasus's stall. This unknown entry in the race had created scarcely any stir. Jake, the undergroom from Devenham who had spent the night there, was able to assure his mistress that the horse was "right as rain" and had "slept a treat" and had munched his oats as calmly as if he'd been back at home. After assuring the groom that "Master

Eustace" would be along in good time for the race, the twosome moved on to Trafalgar's stall, where the situation was quite different.

The groom who had spent the night guarding the big white stallion now eyed a collected crowd with undisguised suspicion and with his barker ill-concealed beneath his coat. But catching the viscount's eye, he gave a reassuring nod to confirm that all was well. Trafalgar arched his neck at just that moment and whinnied lustily, as though playing to the gallery. He seemed every bit as conscious of his featured role as a David Garrick or an Edmund Kean about to go on the stage.

The flash coves in the crowd were much in demand for their opinions before diamond necklaces and carriages were placed at risk. And the experts were generally in accord. The animal was magnificent. It was the rider who was not quite up to snuff.

"Come along, George," Cassandra said quickly before her cousin could hear the general disparagement of his equestrian skill. "It's time we got back to the inn." But as they tried to thread their way outside, they were blocked by an enormous man wearing a broad-brimmed hat, much too high in the crown and far too shiny to be fashionable. He carried a nobbled stick. "Good morning, your ladyship." Mr. Jeremy Gifford bowed awkwardly and removed his regulation headgear.

"Mr. Gifford! What on earth are you doing here?" Cassandra blurted out, then tried for nonchalance. "What an absurd question. All of England is here. There's no reason a Bow Street Runner should not share the mania for horseflesh."

"No, indeed, m'lady. And this particular specimen behind us interests me considerably."

"My cousin's mount? Oh, by the by, George, may I present Mr. Gifford? Think I may have mentioned that he came down to Devenham recently. This is my cousin, Lord Severn."

The viscount fought off a case of the horrors long enough to mumble a shaky greeting. "Mr. G-Gifford."

"Honored, m'lord. As you may know, my reason for going to Devenham Hall was to inquire after your friend Captain the Honorable Charles Danforth."

"Waste of time. The captain's in France. Come along, Cassandra."

"So I've been given to understand." Refusing to be dismissed, Mr. Gifford fell into step beside them as the cousins weaved their way through the crush of bodies and out into the welcome freshness of the open air. "But that is his horse back there that everyone's so interested in."

"Trafalgar, you mean?" George had a sudden flash of inspiration. "It *was* his horse. I bought it. Of course," he added virtuously, "it never occurred to me that he was selling it to finance his flight to France. Still," he went on, getting carried away by a flare for invention he'd never suspected he possessed, "maybe I should have known something was up. Got Trafalgar for a fraction of his worth. Magnificent animal. If I were you, I'd place a guinea or so on him to win. A sure thing, if I do say so myself."

"You will be riding?" The Runner showed a remarkable lack of enthusiasm.

"Of course." George, who hadn't missed as much of the flash coves' expert opinions as Cassandra had wished, looked mulish. "I can't see that the rider has all that much to say to anything. It's the horse that has to jump all those walls and things."

"I quite agree," Mr. Gifford said hastily, while Cassandra interposed, "Did you get a chance to look at Pegasus while you were inside, Mr. Gifford? He's my personal favorite, if my cousin here will forgive my disloyalty. Still, it's all in the family. One of his lordship's younger brothers will be the rider. Take my advice. Put your money on Pegasus."

"Much obliged for the tip, your ladyship. But you see, I never wager." And with that virtuous piece of information, Mr. Gifford made his bow and ambled off in the direction of the steeplechase's starting post.

Cassandra and George hurried back to the inn, where they parted company. But in no time the viscount was tapping on his cousin's door. She opened it a crack and he eased in.

"Will I do?" she asked anxiously as she looked her up and down.

"Egad, no" was the dispiriting reply.

"Well, I don't have my cap on yet." She tried to look at her reflection in the glass objectively. The scarlet hunting coat she wore was loose, fortunately; except for that, it didn't look too bad. She tended to blush when she looked at her limbs, which were tightly encased in buckskins. But, modesty aside, Cassandra reveled in the freedom they afforded. Her hair was piled atop her head in preparation for the concealing cap. "Really, George, I don't see why you're looking so Friday-faced. I think I should get by all right. Why should anyone be especially interested in a rider who's not even supposed to be in the running?"

"It's your cravat. Sit, will you?" He pushed her down on a chair in front of the dressing table.

"My cravat! Who cares about my cravat? Besides, what's wrong with it?"

"Everything." George stood back and squinted into the glass. "I think what you've attempted is the Trône d'Amour, though it's difficult to say. Shouldn't take the field in anything other than an Osbaldistone or a Waterfall. Not de rigueur." He began to unwind the offending neck piece.

"Oh, for heaven's sake, George. My cravat's the very least of my worries. Besides, I saw the messes you wore when Godfrey replaced your Chesney. They looked like something the cat had chewed." Any further disparaging remarks she might have made were forestalled by the deft folds being executed by nimble fingers.

"My word, George, that's beautiful. But I don't understand."

"Simple. After the ghastly experience I had with Charles, I decided never to be caught out again. So I had Chesney spend all last evening teaching me the proper cravat technique. And," he said, preening himself, "he swears he's never had a more apt pupil. Ain't up to his standards, mind you. But still, you'll do. And so will I if Chesney ever does have a mother die or some such thing. I tell you, Cassie, having to go into company with my cravat looking like a sore throat remedy swathed 'round my neck was the worst experience of my life. Up till now.'' He watched critically as his cousin tucked the final strands of her brown hair underneath her hat. ''But something tells me''—he heaved a sigh—''that today's steeplechase is going to make even that horror pale into insignificance.''

Chapter Eighteen

For some time now, on the pretext of looking for Cassan-
dra, Mrs. Alden had been steering Lord Devenham
through the crowd gathered near the starting post while she
scanned it, looking for a shiny hat with an enormous, se-
rious-faced man underneath it. Devenham, who had shown
little enthusiasm for the activity to begin with, was growing
openly rebellious.

"Never could stand crushes," he grumbled. "Come on,
Gwenny. Let's get back to the pavilion. Cassie will know
where to find us. Had no business wandering off, anyway.
Serves her right if she has to stand through the race."

The discouraged Mrs. Alden was just about to resign her
mission when she spied the hat, shining in its glory, above
a crowd of lesser heads. And best of all, quite nearby it,
she spotted three of her London acquaintances.

"Oh, Venetia dear," she called, pulling his lordship with
one hand while parting the way with her parasol clutched
in the other. "How delightful to see you. I don't think

you've met Devenham as yet." She watched the Runner out of the corner of her eye as she loudly made the introductions. At the sound of "Devenham," she was delighted to see the black hat turn her way and sidle a bit nearer.

It was not necessary to introduce the subject of wagering. A fierce debate was already in progress among the elegant London matron and her equally elegant, though considerably younger, male companions. "Venetia dear, I do hope you have your money on Trafalgar," Mrs. Alden whooped at the first opening, projecting her voice toward the Runner's ears.

"Why, no. My blunt's on Plumb. As I should have thought yours would be. Still"—the lady glanced rather slyly at Lord Devenham—"One does find it necessary to occasionally change horses."

"Oh, Plumb knows I'm betting against him this time. You know him. He's not one to mix sentiment with racing. It's never disloyal to bet on the better horse."

"Well"—Lady Venetia Sloop looked doubtfully at her companions—"Winston here does prefer Trafalgar to Thunderer. Perhaps we should change our bet."

"Nonsense!" Lord Devenham was anxious to get back to the pavilion. "Save your blunt. Trafalgar ain't got a chance. Not with my nevvy on him. Nice enough lad, mind you, but—no use mincing words—completely cow-handed when it comes to horses."

"Oh, but, Devenham, did I not tell you?" Excitement, apparently, had turned Mrs. Alden's part of the discourse into a shout. "George won't be riding Trafalgar. His friend Captain Danforth will."

"Danforth!" The ejaculation from the young man who preferred Thunderer almost matched Mrs. Alden's volume. "But that's impossible. The man's gone to France."

"Well, he's not in France now. I have it on the best authority that he'll ride Trafalgar. So if you hurry, you'll still have time to change your wagers."

Mrs. Alden felt the satisfaction that comes to the prophetess who finds her words heeded and acted upon. Her friends scurried to rectify their betting errors before the race began. And a good portion of the crowd within earshot seemed of a similar mind. But, best of all, Mrs. Alden saw Jeremy Gifford moving rapidly away, though not in the direction the crowd was taking. Mr. Gifford's course was toward the starting line.

Gwendolen smiled up at her fiancé, her mission satisfactorily concluded. "Let's go to the pavilion, Devenham. You're right. Cassandra can find us."

"No big rush, actually, m'dear." His lordship was frowning absently. "Think first I'll go and put a pound or so on Trafalgar. To win, of course."

This bit accomplished, they threaded their way to a huge pavilion of bright green silk that glittered with gold cords. Above it flew the flag of England; at lesser heights, all around its borders, flags and buntings of reds and blues and sunshine yellow added gaiety to the scene.

The tent had been erected for the old king's second son, Frederick, Duke of York. But other personages of rank had been invited to join his entourage. Lord Devenham was at a loss to know whether it was his own eminence or his fiancée's popularity that had gained them seats in such company. But his main concern, as they took their places, was his daughter's whereabouts.

"Don't fret about her, Devenham." Mrs. Alden spoke soothingly. "Cassandra probably went to wish Lord Severn and Mr. Davies luck. She can take care of herself."

"That's just the trouble," he grumbled. "She's too deuced good at taking care of herself. She should be here with us in this company." He looked about him at the tonish gathering and noticed a sprinkling of young bucks, apparently unattached. "One reason we came here. To show her off."

At that moment Cassandra was lining up with the other riders and was much too occupied to be bothered by the case of jitters that had plagued her all morning long. Pegasus was now the nervy one. He'd contracted the condition from the other thoroughbreds who were objecting to being held in place in a line and were quivering, stamping, plunging, rearing, kicking. Not to be outdone, Pegasus had attempted a bit of each maneuver before he'd finally settled down in response to a tightly controlled rein, a soothing neck rub, and the murmur of a familiar voice at an unfamiliar pitch.

Now that Pegasus was calmer, Cassandra pulled her cap down even lower and risked a look at the other horsemen. She was relieved to see that the riders on both sides of her were too preoccupied with steadying their own mounts to pay her any heed. She felt a thrill as she looked down the row of scarlet-coated riders, all as well bred as their mounts, the finest horsemen in the land. And in a sudden rush of insight, she faced the truth. It wasn't the money she was after. This steeplechase was not a means to an end. It was the chief end itself—the chance to do what she loved the most and did the best. And to compete on equal terms with these others who shared her passion.

As her eyes traveled down the line, they found their target and saw a troubled pair of blue ones fastened on her. But as their gazes locked, Charlie's worried frown changed to a broad grin of encouragement that caused her throat to constrict suddenly. She beamed back at him.

Behind the line of horses, a somber nemesis was working his way down the row relentlessly, studying each mount and rider as he went. A casual observer might have wondered whether the man in the shiny hat was making a last assessment before wagering. One gentleman whose view he momentarily blocked did shout, "The betting post is closed, sir!" which indeed it was, after a wild, last-minute flurry had made Trafalgar the favorite, while Thunderer had dropped to second place. The horse Pegasus remained a twenty-to-one long shot.

Plumb Davies, second in line as Mr. Gifford began his survey, saw the Runner and relaxed. Gwenny hadn't failed him, after all. Charlie Danforth was about to be pulled from the race. He smiled contentedly. But satisfaction quickly turned to fury as he watched the Runner hesitate behind a prancing, snowy-white stallion and then move slowly on, scrutinizing each new horse and rider closely as he went. The imbecile! Davies screamed silently. The unbelievable fool! The idiot had passed right by Danforth!

Mr. Gifford's intelligence, however, was not at fault. His conscience was the problem. It had been at war within him ever since he'd been singled out by his superiors to attend the Lower Wallop Steeplechase and arrest Captain Danforth if he should have the temerity to show up to ride. Mr. Gifford was a conscientious man of the highest principle. He was proud of a profession that placed him squarely on the right side of the law, while so many of his early neighborhood companions had opted for more questionable livelihoods. When it came to choosing between right and wrong, Jeremy Gifford was not a man to hesitate. The problem in this instance was knowing which was which.

For his sense of gratitude was as finely honed as his sense of duty. And he did not doubt for a minute that had it not been for Captain Danforth, he'd be six feet under in the churchyard now. Still, the man had broken the law. The law that he had sworn to uphold. Therefore, he had no choice.

As he stood behind Trafalgar, Charles, sensing eyes upon him, turned, and the Runner saw the agonized expression on his face. It was then that the Solomonlike solution hit. Jeremy Gifford passed on down the line.

Of course he was honor-bound to bring the captain in. That much was clear. But it boiled down to a matter of timing, that was all. And since in a steeplechase the starting point was also the finish line, well, there was no problem. He could arrest the captain just as readily at the end of the race as at the beginning.

For one brief moment, Mr. Gifford regretted not having placed a small wager on Trafalgar. But he instantly put Satan well behind him. The temptation was unworthy of a member in good standing with the chapel.

Cassandra closed her eyes and took a deep breath to calm herself. And then it came. They were off! The ragged line of horses leaped forward. Shouts from the riders and the crowd swelled to a thunderclap. The Lower Wallop Steeplechase had begun!

The starting line soon broke and quickly re-formed itself into plunging groups. The overeager forged ahead. The more prudent were content with merely setting a good pace while watching the front-runners race one another.

Pegasus strained at the bit, indignant that there were horses up there ahead of him. Cassandra, mindful of Charles's admonition, kept a firm hand on the bridle, refusing to give in to her mount's innate competitiveness and to allow him to lengthen his moderate stride.

They swept across a level and up a slope; as they topped the rise, Cassandra saw in the distance, half a mile away, the first jump: a hedge with a gleam of water just beyond. As the distance between her flying horse and the first hazard closed, in spite of all her mental exhortation, Cassandra felt her mouth go dry. One of the front-runners failed to clear the hedge. His horse went down. She breathed, "Thank God," as the fallen horse lumbered to its feet and walked away while the cursing rider managed to dash to safety before the second pack of horsemen closed in.

The hedge had looked high the day before, the water broad. Now it was Mount Everest, strangely shifted to the edge of the English Channel. "Keep your eyes open for the best takeoff and landing spots." Charles's instructions were burned into her brain. "Steady him about twenty yards from the jump." Just at that point, Pegasus collected his hooves underneath him and went sailing across the hedge and water with graceful ease. Cassandra barely restrained a shout of glee. Why was she so worried? Racing was famous! She was actually having the best time of her life!

Behind her, Charles saw her take the jump safely and breathed a hallelujah of his own. As Trafalgar cleared the hazard, scornful of its lack of challenge, Captain Danforth took himself in hand. This won't do, you know, old man. You've got to win this thing. With a supreme effort of concentration, he managed to wipe Cassandra from his mind. The slight figure on the chestnut was just another rider, one of half a dozen he would eventually have to pass.

Once the twenty-four scarlet-clad centaurs had topped the rise and disappeared from view, the spectators in the pavilion began to mill around and to socialize while champagne corks popped and picnic hampers were unpacked.

"I can't imagine what's become of Cassandra," his lordship remarked for the dozenth time.

"Perhaps she's joined someone in a carriage and is racing to another vantage point herself," Mrs. Alden reassured him. "You know how sport-minded she is."

"Only too well." His lordship's voice lacked enthusiasm. He tried another question he'd also worn threadbare. "Are you sure, Gwenny, that it was Charles Danforth on the big white horse?"

"Quite sure." She could not imagine what had gone wrong. Still, it was Plumb's problem now. She had done her part.

"Well, I don't see what all the fuss is about," he grumbled, thinking of his ten-pound wager. "Didn't seem to get off to a particularly good start."

"Perhaps that was merely strategy. Charlie's a fly one."

"Think so?" He sounded doubtful. "Well, the race ain't always to the swift, they say. By the by, Gwenny, how did you find out Danforth was riding? Thought the hue and cry was out for him."

"Oh"—she dimpled over the rim of the wine goblet a liveried footman had just handed her—"I got it right from the horse's mouth. You see, I happen to know where Charlie's been hiding all this time."

"Do you, by Jove! Where?"

"Devenham Hall."

His lordship looked thunderstruck. "Come now, Gwenny," he blurted out when he'd recovered, "don't fun with me."

"I'm not funning. He really was at Devenham."

"You mean when that Runner cove came down, we actually had a fugitive hiding in the hall?"

She nodded.

"My God!" He sat down suddenly. "Tell me, did Cassandra know?"

"Why, yes." She pulled another gilt chair up beside him. "Well, not to say 'know,' exactly. Though I do think she must eventually have had her suspicions. And do you know, Devenham," she said thoughtfully, "unless I miss my guess, your daughter is a bit in love with Charles Danforth."

"Cassie in love with a criminal? I won't have it!"

"Oh, I'd not call Charlie a criminal," she said, patting his hand soothingly. "The only thing he's guilty of is faulty judgment, an excess of loyalty." She then went on to elaborate. At the end of her explanation, Lord Devenham's only comment was a thoughtful, prolonged "Harrumph!"

Chapter Nineteen

*E*ven as he concentrated on guiding Thunderer over an acre of ground made treacherous by recent plowing, Plumb Davies continued to assess the field. Like Captain Danforth, he realized the necessity of husbanding his horse's strength for the final push. He paid little attention to the sprinkling of riders well up ahead. Carnaby, for instance, was notorious as a poor finisher. O'Hara was already falling back. These flashes in the pan were not his enemies. He was well aware that Danforth was there behind him, finding anonymity in the pack. For the moment, Charlie seemed content to maintain a steady pace. Davies wouldn't worry about him yet. He turned his attention to the unknown quantity who rode just two lengths ahead, practically abreast with three other riders.

Mr. Davies had been watching the chestnut for some time now. There was something familiar about the animal, but to his knowledge he'd never seen the rider before. Mentally, he ran through the list of entries, most of whom he'd ridden against countless times. Severn's younger brother was on that list. He'd dismissed the lad as negligible, he recalled. Now he watched the chestnut sail over the fence with ease. Remarkable thing if a near relative of George Severn could ride like that. This lad would have to be dealt with first, Plumb concluded as he in turn went soaring through the air, before he could get on with the crucial task of beating Charles Danforth.

Cassandra tried to keep her mind off the casualties as the miles were eaten up and more and more riders were eliminated by the hazards. But even the furious drumming of hooves could not drown out the agonizing sounds as men and horses failed to make the jumps. She set her jaw grimly and rode on. A stretch of level, fallow ground gave her an opportunity to glance back. The field was thinning fast. Yes, Charlie was still back there, cool and nonchalant, riding as if on a Sunday outing. He raised his whip in a salute when he saw her head turn. She quickly pulled her attention back to where it belonged.

Plumb Davies rode just half a length behind her. For some time now she'd been aware of his assessing stare. He seemed to be pacing his horse with hers, studying Pegasus to discover what he was up against. The hairs on her neck prickled from his scrutiny.

At that moment, Cassandra came close to panic. Plumb Davies was sticking like a leach; Charles spelled disaster, waiting to overtake her. She was just about to use her spurs and leave the unnerving twosome far behind when "Remember . . . it's the last half mile that counts" came floating before her eyes like the Holy Writ.

Foot by foot, yard by yard, the race went on. A gray passed Danforth and Plumb Davies, gaining on Cassandra. She kept tight control of Pegasus, fighting his urge to meet the other horse's challenge. The gray was breathing heavily as it pulled ahead. Cassandra ducked lower still over Pegasus's mane to dodge the flying clods tossed up by the pounding hooves.

As they approached a ditch, Davies's sorrel still maintained its steady pace behind her. The winded gray ahead faltered just before the jump, then didn't make it. Pegasus cleared the hazard while the gray struggled to rise on a broken leg. Cassandra battled a wave of nausea, trying to wipe the picture from her mind. Plumb Davies chose that moment to pull even with her.

"What a delightful surprise, your ladyship!" he shouted, raising his riding crop in a mock salute. Only then did Cassandra realize that she'd lost her cap. Her hair was loose and streaming as she rode.

"You ride well, m'dear," the taunting voice continued, "but you do realize, I hope, that chivalry can play no part in a steeplechase. This is where we divide the men from the, er, 'boys.' " And with an exultant cry and a flick of his crop, Davies urged Thunderer into the lead.

"Now!" Cassandra commanded, and set out after him. They cleared another ditch, with Pegasus on the sorrel's heels, and went flying down a slope, both riders with their knees in and their heads held low. At the foot of the hill, Cassandra drew abreast and raced Davies neck and neck. Their horses might have been the only entries in the field. As they passed first one and then another of the three front-runners, they had no thought left for anybody else. The race had narrowed down to two straining, foam-flecked horses, each determined to best the other or perish in the attempt.

Behind them, Charles had watched Davies throw down the gauntlet. He lengthened Trafalgar's stride and closed in a few lengths behind the flying pair. His former single-minded concentration was totally destroyed. He watched the duel with a cold rush of fear for the inexperienced rider running spur to spur with the wily veteran. Oh, dear lord, the wall! He broke into a clammy sweat.

Cassandra, too, was well aware of the danger up ahead as the horses galloped in tandem, narrowing the distance between themselves and the worst hazard of the course. Before them loomed a high brick wall, too high to jump except for one place where the bricks had crumbled away to leave a gap barely wide enough to accommodate one horse and rider.

"Give way!" Davies shouted in their headlong rush.

"You give way! I'm half a head in front!"

"Never!" was the answer, and Cassandra, who knew he meant it, balanced the odds and at the final moment pulled her mount and let Davies take the jump just ahead of her. Pegasus, thrown off his stride, flicked off a brick with a flying hoof, then stumbled in the landing, but he managed to regain his balance and surge forward, determined to close the gap that now existed between himself and his hated rival.

"Thank God," Charles breathed as he cleared the wall, and saw Pegasus maintain his footing and regain his speed.

The race is just now beginning. Cassandra grimly reminded herself of Charles's last instruction. They were entering the final phase. Davies had forced her hand a bit too soon. And she was well aware of Trafalgar bearing down on them from behind. But never mind. Pegasus was no ordinary horse. She sensed no tiredness in the beast, only exhilaration, as he closed in on his rival and drew abreast.

Davies cursed and flailed at Thunderer with his whip. The sorrel responded. But Pegasus hung on like a leech and matched him stride for stride. Before them gleamed a water jump and, just beyond, a hedge. And after that a stretch of smooth turf ran up a hill and back down to the finish line.

Like Cassandra, Davies was aware of Trafalgar close behind. And he did not for a minute doubt that there was where the real threat lay. Danforth's holding back, he thought, waiting to see which of us can beat the other. Well, then, I'll oblige him.

They were bearing down on the water jump, still dead even, with only a yard's distance between the speeding steeds. Just as Cassandra marked her spot and readied Pegasus for the takeoff, Davies roweled his horse savagely, gave a shout, and swerved Thunderer directly at his rival.

"Look out!" Charles yelled behind him, but his warning could not be heard above the thundering hooves. Cassandra saw the danger, though, and managed to swing Pegasus aside just in time to avoid being ridden down. The horse, thus balked, made a brave attempt but could not complete the jump and landed short, missing the dry ground and going down with a floundering splash. Charles, sailing over the water hazard just behind them, saw that Cassandra had been thrown clear. He soared over the water jump, then spurted across the short open space that led to the hedge and jumped it. Now only Davies and one other rider were left between him and the finish line. He focused on Thunderer and his jockey through a red glare of hate.

Dizzy, wet, covered and half-blinded with muck and slime, Cassandra staggered to her feet, dimly aware that other horses were galloping down upon them and leaping past, missing them by mere inches. All of her dazed attention was upon Pegasus as he heaved himself out of the mire and scrambled for solid footing. Cassandra just managed to grab his bridle to pull him out of the path of a lunging bay. Pegasus whinnied impatiently at her, resenting the delay and ready to join the race again. But once out of the danger from other stragglers, Cassandra buried her face against her horse's flank and burst into tears.

The rider of the bay horse, having safely cleared the water jump, was focusing his attention on the hedge when a big white horse came leaping back across it straight into his path. "You damn fool! You're headed the wrong way!" whooped the bay's rider as Charles Danforth met him. "Have you gone stark mad?"

"Yes!" the other shouted in reply as he swerved away toward the mud-covered horse and its grieving rider.

Charles jumped off Trafalgar, took Cassandra by the shoulders, and turned her around gently. "Are you all right?"

The tears were coursing down her face, tracing intricate patterns of rivulets through the muck. She gulped and nodded, unable to reply.

"Well, then, that's all that matters." He folded her, pond scum and all, into his arms and patted her consolingly on the back, while she hiccoughed and snuffled against his shoulder. "There, there now. Steeplechasers don't cry. It's another one of the rules I forgot to tell you. No need to take it so hard. You ran a damn fine race. I was proud of you."

She raised her head from his shoulder then to look up at him with wide, staring eyes. "You aren't just saying that to make me feel better, are you? Do you really mean it, Godfrey?"

"Absolutely." He cleaned the mud tenderly from her lips with his fingertips. "Couldn't have done better myself. Didn't, in fact," he added ruefully.

Then Cassandra awakened to reality. While she had been leaning against Pegasus, dazed, all her hopes shattered by her fall, it had seemed only natural that Godfrey—Charles—was there to comfort her. Now she was horrified. "What are you doing here? You were right behind me. You made the water jump. I saw you."

"Well, I had to see that you were all right, didn't I?"

"No! No!" Now she was furious with him. She pounded her fists on his chest. "You should have gone on. You could have beaten that—that—that—"

"Bastard?" he supplied helpfully.

"At least. Did you see what that—that—that—that what you called him did to me?"

"I saw," he answered grimly. "That's one reason I came back. I felt responsible. For when I was handing out all my sage advice, I forgot to tell you the most important thing: It's not enough just to ride well. You have to realize the other coves are the Enemy."

"He couldn't have beaten me fairly. Not in a million years. My horse was better, and he knew it. Oh, Charles," she said, her voice filled with anguish, "do you realize that—that—that what you called him has probably won?"

"Undoubtedly. But then that's life. You almost never find a well-aimed thunderbolt turning up where it's most needed." He had walked over to Pegasus and was running skillful hands over the horse's legs and withers. "Well," he said cheerfully, "it could be a lot worse. Looks like you and Pegasus both came out of the wars unscathed.

Now I think we'd both better make ourselves scarce. Those people over there''—he nodded toward a distant group of spectators staring their way curiously—''will be sending out a scouting party to check on stragglers. Here, put this on.'' He removed his mud-splattered cap and handed it to Cassandra. ''Tuck up your hair and get to the stables. You should be able to make it safely back to the inn while Davies is collecting his laurel wreath. Then no one need ever know that the very proper Lady Cassandra Devenham rode in the gentlemen's steeplechase.''

He helped her into the saddle. ''But aren't you coming, too?'' she asked as he turned Trafalgar in the opposite direction.

''I'm afraid not. There's a Bow Street reception committee waiting for me at the finish line.''

''Oh, how awful! I hadn't thought. Here I've been feeling sorry for myself, and it's much, much worse for you. Oh, Charles, what have I done to you?''

''Lord only knows.'' He grinned crookedly. ''There'll be time enough to assess the damage when I'm well away from here. Right now I'd best get started.''

''But where will you be going?''

''Oh, God!'' This was another question Charles Danforth was loath to deal with. But the answer to this one couldn't be postponed. ''To France.'' He sighed. ''I've gone to no end of trouble to avoid the place, but now it looks like I've got no other choice. Just as well, perhaps.'' His eyes narrowed. ''While I'm there, I intend to look up an old regimental chum of mine. Godspeed, m'lady.'' He raised his whip in farewell and broke into a gallop.

Cassandra sat watching till the big white horse and rider had vanished over the hill. Then she wiped her eyes with the backs of her grimy hands and, turning Pegasus, rode swiftly toward the stables.

Chapter Twenty

A cheer rose as *Plumb Davies came galloping down* the stretch, his heaving horse flecked with foam and blood from whip and spurs. The cheers were immediately drowned by groans when a keen-eyed watcher bellowed, "It's Mr. Davies riding Thunderer! Thunderer's the winner!"

"Where the devil's Trafalgar?" Lord Devenham, on tip-toe in the pavilion, could have spoken for the majority of spectators who had bet on Captain Danforth's skill and reputation. But if his question was addressed to Mrs. Alden, it missed the mark. For that lady had left his side to push through the throng collected around the winner and to hurl herself into Plumb Davies's arms. The crowd tittered nervously as the victor kissed the lady long and ardently. It was not until the Duke of York harrumphed politely in the background that the couple parted and allowed Davies to receive the royal commendation.

Devenham watched the scene with a stony expression.

He would definitely have to have a word with Gwendolen about her conduct. Tying her garters in public this way! It was not at all the thing. Lest he, too, give way publicly to his own emotions, his lordship turned on his heel and left the pavilion, more than a little disenchanted with the sport of kings. And where was Cassandra, anyhow? Well, by George, she could find her own way back to the inn. Provided she'd shown up for the race, that is. And when it came to that, let Gwendolen find her own way back as well. She'd not want for escorts, that was certain. Somehow, Lord Devenham was not as pleased with his lady's popularity as he once had been.

Once safely ensconced in a bedchamber of the Fighting Cock, Lord Devenham, that man of action, made an uneasy foray into thought. He did not find the terrain hospitable. Too many things had been shoved to the back of his mind for too long. And certain recent disclosures added to his discomfort. A knock on the door was a welcome release from this uneasy cogitation.

An inn servant handed him a note. Lord Devenham gave the man a vail, then sat back down on his bed to smooth out the pleated paper. The letter's contents brought on a further bout of thought, though of shorter duration. "Oh, the devil take 'em!" he exclaimed. His lordship sounded more relieved than angry as he jumped up and strode purposefully from the room.

The knock on Cassandra's door had all the force of the clap of doom. "Just a minute." Still dripping from the hip bath, she shoved her muddy riding clothes out of sight and reached for her dressing gown. Her face was pale in the afternoon sunshine, the pallor not all due to the removal of the evidence of her fall. Her freshly washed hair hung damply on her shoulders and her feet were bare as she opened the chamber door.

"Let's go home, Cassandra," her father barked. "No need to stay on here. Of course, if you want to," he added as an afterthought, "you could always go back with George. Nothing improper about it. Good as betrothed."

If it had been possible, more color would have drained from Cassandra's face. "No, I'd rather go with you, sir."

"Good. We'll leave in half an hour."

Cassandra did not keep him waiting. She was neatly attired in a gray bombazine dress, with her dampened hair tucked under a velour bonnet, when their crested carriage came swinging around to the Fighting Cock's door. As her father handed her inside, she looked around her. They were not the only ones bent on an early exit. Other carriages were being loaded with disgruntled passengers forced to abandon the hospitality of the inn ahead of schedule, their pockets now to let. Conversely, the sound of revelry drifted out from the public room where a celebration by those fortunates who had backed Thunderer at odds was now in progress.

"Where's Mrs. Alden?" Cassandra inquired as her father signaled the coachman to spring his horses.

"She's staying on." There was something in her father's tone that discouraged further questioning. Besides, she was too blue-deviled to be curious, only grateful to escape the social chatter.

But when they'd left the village a mile or so behind, Lord Devenham broke the silence. "Might as well tell you, I suppose. Gwenny won't be coming. Ever. She's run off with that Davies cove."

"Mrs. Alden and Plumb Davies! Papa, are you serious?"

"Of course I'm serious," he snapped. "Damn fool question. No fit subject for a joke. Should have suspected something of the kind when she plastered herself all over him after he'd won that blasted race." He paused and frowned. "Should have suspected something long before that, now I come to think on it.

"Anyhow," he resumed his exposition, "she left a note. Said they'd always loved each other but couldn't do anything about it since between 'em they hadn't a feather to fly with. Now that he's won so heavily—played deep, she said, the both of 'em"—he groaned for his own losses—"they're off to France."

Cassandra spared a moment to consider the new boom in tourism that the French were enjoying. Would the elopers and Charles Danforth perhaps cross on the same packet? Then she roused herself to say, "Oh, Papa, I'm so sorry."

"Well, I ain't!" Lord Devenham spoke with true conviction. "Been thinking for some time that we wouldn't suit. Can you believe that Gwenny actually wanted to be in London during the hunting season?"

"No! How terrible." In spite of everything, Cassandra barely suppressed a smile.

"Good riddance is what I call it."

"Well, then, I'm happy for you."

Father and daughter lapsed into silence once again. Cassandra seemed to be fascinated by the view outside her carriage window, but actually she was oblivious to the pretty thatched cottage where a pair of black-and-white cattle cropped the grass. She was trying to find a tactful way to break her bad news and couldn't. She gave it up, swallowed hard, then summoned her courage and spoke straight to the point. "I'm not marrying George, either, Papa. That was all a big misunderstanding. I'm sorry." She braced herself for the explosion that was sure to follow.

It didn't come. A rather mild "Harrumph" was the only comment.

And it seemed to convey an amazing amount of tolerance and understanding. Both Devenhams resumed their meditation. But now his lordship had been diverted from his own heartburnings. "Tell me," he asked after a bit, "that fellow, Captain Danforth. Gwendolen said you knew all along that he was at the hall."

Devenham was no master of the art of subtlety. He was fishing for a confession, Cassandra realized. Unfortunately, she mistook the nature of the admission he expected.

"Well, yes, I did know." Cassandra's face filled with misery. "I mean, I didn't know who he actually was till the Runner came looking for him. I simply thought he was a most peculiar valet. And I thought it decidedly odd that he kept putting his horse through such strange maneuvers. And then it all came together—the fact that he was hiding out, waiting to ride in the steeplechase. And then, Papa, I did a terrible thing.'' The story came pouring out, of how she'd used this knowledge to blackmail Captain Danforth and her cousin George into helping her enter the steeplechase.

At the end of her recital, Lord Devenham sat mute. For there were no words to convey his horror. Cassandra watched him with alarm; still, some imp of pride goaded her into adding, ''Papa, I would have won if that—that—villain, Davies, hadn't swerved into Pegasus at the water jump.''

''Thank God for it!''

''Thank God? That Pegasus could have been lamed? Or my neck broken?'' Indignation had taken over her common sense. ''You're *thankful?*''

''By Jupiter, I am! That's the second good turn that rascal Davies has done me. He's stolen Gwenny and he's kept you from disgracing the proud name of Devenham. When I think that it could've been you galloping up to the Duke of York . . .'' He shuddered. ''I tell you it don't bear thinking on. I owe that Davies more than I can say. Damn if I begrudge a penny of that wager that he cost me!''

''I thought you might have been proud of me, Papa. After all, you're the one who taught me to ride.''

''Well, I never dreamed you'd do a rackety thing like enter a gentlemen's steeplechase, now, did I? If word of that ever gets out . . . Are you sure no one recognized you?''

''I don't think so.'' She was well past caring.

''Well, if even I thought you was Eustace when the field was lining up, I don't suppose any of the other spectators knew the difference. But I tell you now, Cassandra, if you ever do such a scandalous thing again . . . Damme, your Aunt Amelia was right, after all. Never should've let you join those hunts I gave. 'No female does that sort of thing,' she told me—a hundred times at least, I swear it—'except for the Marchioness of Salisbury, who's more man than woman, anyhow.' So I suppose I'll have to share some of the blame myself," he concluded magnanimously. "It all just goes to prove one thing. The sooner you're settled, the better it will be for all concerned."

Then Lord Devenham closed his eyes to study the problem. But soon, what with the swaying of the coach and the melodious squeaking of the left rear wheel, he was lulled into the twilight of sleep only to be jerked awake immediately as their coachman swerved to make way for a speeding vehicle to pass them.

"Who were those imbeciles?" Lord Devenham roared as a curricle tooled skillfully by on the narrow road. "Damned Corinthians!" He shook his fist at the vanishing backs of two gentlemen as one of them cracked his whip out over the perfectly matched team of grays and produced an even greater burst of speed. "Let 'em break their own damned necks if they want to. No need to put innocent travelers in the ditch!"

Cassandra did not comment. Indeed, she could not. For unlike her dozing parent, she had gotten a good look at the two young men hell-bent on arriving quickly at their destination. She was immensely relieved when Devenham leaned back once more and reclosed his eyes.

What she could not know was that there was no real need for her father to speculate further on the identity of the speedsters. As so often happens in a moment of alarm, he had actually seen more than he at first realized. A picture of the bright red spokes and matching leather of his nephew George's equipage was storehoused in his consciousness along with the beginnings of a Machiavellian scheme just before it surrendered itself once more to Morpheus.

When the carriage pulled up before the entrance to the hall, Lord Devenham and Cassandra both had a single thought and pressing need: to talk to Charles Danforth. But since his lordship felt no compulsion to be circumspect and marched straight up to the Viscount Severn's room, Cassandra, slipping down the hall a little later, found herself forestalled. When she heard her father peremptorily dismiss George, who was rummaging through his things to unearth what cash and valuables he could find to finance his friend's journey, she dashed back into her chamber out of her cousin's sight, then shamelessly returned to her post to eavesdrop.

It wasn't easy. The thick portals at Devenham had been built for privacy. She held her breath and cracked the door a bit. The two men inside were too engrossed in conversation to notice their exposure.

"Owe you an apology for abusing your hospitality, sir," Charles was saying. "But frankly there ain't time to make it properly. There's a Runner from Bow Street on my heels."

"I know all about that," his lordship replied impatiently. "And why you ever were fool enough to sign a note held by that cent-per-center Grimes is more than I can say. The man's a bloodsucker."

"I'm well aware of that, sir. Just didn't think Lewison would leave me holding the bag. Besides, I fully expected a windfall."

"The race, you mean. Well, ah, yes. That was bad luck." His lordship cleared his throat in embarrassment. "Should've won, I understand. And that's what I want to talk to you about. I say, m'boy, this ain't what you might call easy. Could you stop all that for a minute and just listen?" The conversation had been accompanied by the sound of boots rapidly walking to and fro and the thud of various items landing in or near a portmanteau.

"Sorry, your lordship. But time is of the essence."

"No, it ain't. Not necessarily. That's what this is all about. I know, you see, that my daughter was the cause of your losing the steeplechase. At least everybody said you were a sure thing. Lost a few pounds on you myself." There was regret in his voice.

"Very sorry, sir."

"But that's neither here nor there. The thing is, I'm prepared to pay off your debt. On one condition." There was a silence inside while Cassandra held her breath.

"And what's that, sir?" The captain's expressionless voice filled the void.

"That you marry my Cassandra."

She felt the blood surge to her head. She had to grasp the door frame for support. She wanted to scream her protest but found herself struck dumb.

This time the pause was interminable. Finally, "Do I understand you correctly, sir? You are offering me a thousand pounds to wed Cassandra?"

"Yes. Immediately. We can decide on the rest of the settlement later. I know I've caught you off guard, but when you think on it, the idea makes sense. You're in a coil. And it's time the gel was married. More than time, in fact." Lord Devenham choked a bit. "My God! Riding in a steeplechase! Of all the rackety—Well, never mind." He got himself under control again. "Marriage to the right man would put a period to that sort of thing. George wants her, as you probably know, but frankly, I don't think the lad can handle her. Cassie's headstrong. I won't mislead you there. But from what I hear you should be able to keep a tight rein on her. Besides, Mrs. Alden thinks she's in love with you."

Cassandra had not thought it possible to feel worse. But she was wrong. She leaned her head against the doorjamb and prayed for death.

Again, the reply was slow in coming. "Gwenny said that, did she?"

"Yes, and she should know." His lordship's voice held more than a trace of bitterness. "She's an expert on that sort of thing. So how about it, lad? It's a simple enough thing. I pay your debt. You marry Cassie. Will you do it?"

"No."

The flat syllable hung in the air. Then the sound of hasty packing resumed.

Cassandra waited to hear no more but fled silently back to her chamber and flung herself across her bed. It was not until she heard the familiar sound of a pair of boots striding down the hall, clattering down the stairs, and fading into silence that she allowed the tears to flow.

Lady Cassandra was up early the next morning, composed if pale. She found her father in the breakfast room spreading Quodeny of Plum over a lavishly buttered wig. "Oh, good," he said thickly through an enormous bite, "it's you. Very person I need to see. Can you let our houseguests know the wedding's off, then shoo them out? I'm ready, b'gad, to get back to normal."

Normal. That one word separated from the others and seemed to mock her. Cassandra wondered if her blighted world would ever be "normal" again.

"Very well, Papa." Actually, she sounded quite normal herself, she noted. "Once everyone's up, I'll see to it. But first I have a favor to ask. I need a thousand pounds."

"For lord's sake, Cassie." He groaned. "You ain't going to start up again about your own establishment. It's not necessary any longer. The two of us can rub along just as we always—Oh. A thousand pounds, you say?" The coincidence of the amount suddenly struck Lord Devenham.

"Yes, Papa. I wish to pay off Captain Danforth's debt. I feel responsible, you see, for the coil he's in. If it had not been for me—" She almost lost her calm control but with an effort of will managed to rally. "If it weren't for me, he would have won the race and cleared himself. And he hates the thought of France."

Her father was looking puzzled. "I don't understand you at all, girl. You said you expected to win that race. Don't happen to think myself you could have pulled the thing off. Not in a million years. Oh, you're a damned fine rider, if I do say so, but still and all, a woman, don't you know. But for the sake of argument, let's say you had won. Well, things would be no different then than they are right now. Danforth still couldn't pay and would have to take to his heels."

"Yes, but you see, I didn't know then why the Bow

Street Runner was after Captain Danforth. If I had known, I'd never have entered and tried to beat him."

"Just what did you think he was guilty of?" Lord Devenham was curious as to the type of criminal his daughter could fall in love with.

Her face grew warm. "I'm afraid I just assumed it had to do with a woman. The likelihood seemed that he'd been caught in some female's bed by an irate husband and then forced to fight an illegal duel. Something of the kind. The captain does have a certain reputation as a . . . ." She faltered over the proper terminology.

"Rake?"

"I was about to say 'beau.' 'Rake,' no doubt, is the better choice. But my speculations are quite beside the point, Father. The point is, when I entered the race I didn't know that Captain Danforth was an innocent victim and liable for someone else's debt. And I did keep him from winning and paying the moneylender. So now I want to make things right."

"Hmmm." Lord Devenham studied his daughter's face but could make little of it. "I ain't as averse to the idea as you might suppose, Cassie. The truth is, I'm plain grateful to the captain for not winning. I don't mind saying again that I'm damned relieved that Davies could afford to run off with Gwenny. But the thing is, you see"—he looked uncomfortable—"I offered Danforth the money myself and he wouldn't take it. Too proud to accept charity, I collect."

"But this time, Papa, there will be no strings attached."

"Beg pardon?"

"This time Captain Danforth will not be required to marry me."

Her father reddened slowly. "How the devil did you find out?"

"I was listening."

"Well! I must say!" he sputtered. "Of all the shabby—dishonorable—"

"Not so dishonorable as offering your daughter for sale, Papa. But let's not wander off the subject except to say that

178

I think a thousand pounds is a small price to ask for the humiliation you cost me. Besides, I don't expect you to make a gift of the money. Captain Danforth's prospects are quite good, I understand. I'm sure you'll get your money back. Will you do it?''

A crafty light came into her parent's eyes. ''Hmmm. And if I do, will you agree not to mention wanting your own establishment anymore?''

''Yes, Papa. I agree.''

''Good.'' He slathered butter onto another wig. ''Now go on, Cassie, and clear the hall of company. I'm more than ready to be comfortable again.''

Chapter Twenty-one

*T*he Clarges Street office of Grimes the moneylender was
experiencing a rush of business. The Viscount Severn
had been the first to arrive. Now he was arguing with the
cent-per-center, a tubby, balding man whose benign
expression belied his reputation.

"What do you mean you won't take the money from
me? Solid English currency? My God!" The viscount
looked appalled. "Don't tell me you're holding out for a
pound of flesh!" Lord Severn had been the despair of all
his tutors, none more so than the one who had sought to
acquaint him with the Bard. It would have amazed the
scholar to learn that a bit of seed had fallen on good ground.

The moneylender was too accustomed to dealing with
the nobility to take offense. "Nothing like that, m'lord,"
he replied patiently. "The thing is, I've had a communi-
cation from Captain Danforth. He's raising the money himself and on no account am I to take it from anyone else."

"But blast it, man, he's gone to France."

At that moment Lord Devenham, accompanied against his will by his daughter, entered the loan establishment and recognized the voice in the inner office. Ignoring an ink-stained young clerk who insisted that Mr. Grimes should not be disturbed, the earl barged in, with Cassandra in his wake.

"What the devil are you doing here, George?" Devenham thundered. "Don't tell me you've fallen into this bloodsucker's clutches."

"Of course not." George looked offended. "Fact is, I was about to ask you the same question." But as his uncle's choler began to mount, he quickly added, "Actually, I'm here to pay off Charlie's debt. But Grimes here"—he jerked a thumb at the moneylender, who had risen courteously when Devenham and Cassandra entered—"says he won't take my money. Says Charlie sent 'round a note that he's raising the blunt. Surely he didn't put the touch on you, did he? Makes no sense. I've known him longer. Still, Charlie don't believe in borrowing from his friends, and you ain't one."

"Oh, do be quiet, George." Devenham turned to Grimes. "I'm prepared to settle Captain Danforth's debts for him here and now."

"That will not be acceptable."

The quartet in the inner office was jerked around by a voice from the open doorway. Its tone was aristocratic, authoritative, and decidedly on the cool side. "I do not know the reason for your generosity, sir," the newcomer continued, "nor do I inquire about it. But I will not allow you to make such a sacrifice on my son's behalf. Captain Danforth's profligacy is a family matter." He joined the ring around the moneylender's desk.

There was no mistaking Charles Danforth's father. The height, the features carried an undeniable stamp. Age had silvered the hair. A streak of sternness, lacking in the offspring, accounted for the toplofty expression. Still, Cassandra felt as if she were gazing into a crystal ball to see Charles thirty years from then.

"If you will apprise me of my son's indebtedness, sir"—the imperious gaze focused on Grimes—"I will settle it."

For the first time, Mr. Grimes appeared uneasy. He could deal with the other toffs. This one was of a different stamp entirely. "Begging your lordship's pardon, but I've had strict instructions from the captain not to take the money from anyone but him. He wishes to pay me himself."

Lord Meredith spoke dryly. "For a person who depends upon usury for a livelihood, you appear overly particular about the sources of your money, sir. My son seems to have anticipated the generosity of his friends." His cool eyes scanned each of the others in the room, pausing rather longer on Cassandra, and then returned to Grimes. "While it does him credit not to shift the burden of his debts to other shoulders, the fact remains that if you wait for my son to pay you, sir, you may have to whistle for it."

"That's hard, m'lord." It was the debtor himself who now stood in the doorway, gazing reproachfully at his sire. "Shows a want of proper paternal feeling, if I may say so. Not to mention a devilish lack of faith."

Cassandra, whose knees had suddenly weakened—a chronic condition that the sight of Captain Danforth seldom failed to trigger—sat down in the only chair, except for Grimes's, the office offered. Charles, she decided, had never appeared to better advantage. He had obviously been reunited with his wardrobe, for the dark blue superfine coat he wore fitted his broad shoulders to perfection. His pearl-gray pantaloons encased his well-formed legs with a snug adherence that seemed to defy his knees to bend.

The knees triumphed nonetheless, for Captain Danforth crossed the small room in three jaunty strides and threw a bulging purse down on Grimes's battered desk. "It's all there. Count it." The words, though addressed to Grimes, were for his father's benefit. "I'll need a receipt, of course."

"Oh, I say! This won't do, you know!" Six pairs of eyes turned simultaneously to view the latest entry in the doorway.

"My word, it's Lewison!" The Viscount Severn gasped.

A slightly built young man, wearing the uniform of the Household Brigade, regarded the assemblage through guileless eyes. His curly ginger hair and side whiskers gave the officer a decided dash. His smile was cordial to the extreme. But it found no answering warmth in the expressions of those in the little group who knew him. Captain Danforth, for example, was surveying the newcomer with a frosty demeanor quite worthy of his father.

"Where the devil have you been?" barked Severn.

"To Paris. On my wedding trip."

"Your wedding trip!" George exclaimed. His uncle thought fleetingly of his own deliverance from a similar excursion.

"That's right. Eloped, you see."

"*Decamped*, you mean." There was no obvious softening of the viscount's disapproval.

"Nothing of the kind. Couldn't get Sir Wilfred Coxe's permission to wed his daughter, don't you see." (The moneylender's eyes grew wide at the mention of one of the nation's foremost nabobs.) "So had no choice. Meant to come back a bit sooner, old sport," he addressed Charles apologetically. "But, well, you know how it goes with a honeymoon. Or can imagine it, at any rate. One does tend to lose all track of time. I hope I haven't inconvenienced you, old man."

"Inconvenienced me?" Charles's newly acquired veneer of hauteur began to crack. "Inconvenienced me?" His face split into a grin. "Oh, not at all, Lewison, old chap." He leaned weakly against the wall and began to laugh.

"Well, here's your money, Grimes." The officer laid his offering on the lender's desk, then turned an anxious eye on Charles. He seemed to fear for his old comrade-in-arm's sanity. "Here, catch!" He tossed the captain's purse to Danforth, who plucked it out of the air. "Got to run now. Christobel's holding the horses. Matched bays! Prime high-steppers! Like to see 'em, Charlie?"

Captain Danforth, whose shoulders were still inclined to shake, shook his head as well.

"Oh, well. Some other time, then. Can't thank you

enough, Charlie, old man. Well, must run. Good day, all.'' Captain Lewison bowed himself out of the room.

"Let's go, too, Papa," Cassandra murmured, not trusting herself to look at Charles, who had taken a step toward her but found his way blocked by his father.

"I think you and I should have a talk, my boy." Lord Meredith was incapable of appearing shamefaced. He was, however, decidedly less overbearing. "White's suit you?"

Viscount Severn gave a cool nod to the moneylender and then hurried to catch up with his uncle and Cassandra. But he was waylaid by an insistent Lewison, eager for someone to admire his team and to meet his bride. And before George could extricate himself from those two treats, his uncle's curricle, with Cassandra holding the reins, went sweeping past and disappeared around the corner.

As he walked on down the street where his tiger was guarding his high perch phaeton, George wondered at the ironies of fate. Imagine Lewison, whose pockets had been constantly to let, eloping with an heiress. His new equipage reeked of money. As did his horses. As did his bride. Old Lewison had landed on his feet, all right. But at what price? Matrimony! The very word caused the bachelor to shudder as he climbed up onto the leather seat, thankfully alone.

In the last several days, Lady Cassandra had changed old habits. She had taken up riding in the evening on the theory that a different time would make her mind less prone to dwell upon those rides with Charles. She was experiencing indifferent success.

Now a haze hung over the valley between the rolling hills as nature drowsed in the last of the day's sunshine. The black-and-white cattle seemed too lethargic to move out of the way as Pegasus weaved among them. They chewed their cuds soporifically and eyed the horse and rider with little interest. All of nature, including Pegasus, seemed to echo Cassandra's blue-deviled mood. For once, the horse was content to move along slowly, as unenthusiastic with this day's outing as his mistress.

But at the sound of fast-approaching hoofbeats, his ears

pricked up. He shook his mane and whinnied away his apathy. Cassandra turned to look behind her and saw a big white horse rapidly bearing down upon them. It's as well I'm sitting down, she thought inanely, recalling the usual reaction of her knees to such a sighting. This was to be her last clear thought for some time to come.

Pegasus, recognizing a challenge when he heard it, was swept back to his recent glory days. It was the steeplechase at Lower Wallop all over again. He stretched his legs and took off like the wind as he felt the hot breath of Trafalgar upon his flank.

The white horse closed in, and they went plummeting down the hillside, neck and neck; then Pegasus swerved and went racing through the grassy valley with Trafalgar at his side. Just what the eventual outcome might have been was anybody's guess. For the ex-cavalry officer, displaying considerable skill and considerably more diplomacy, leaned low, managed to catch his rival's bridle, and pull both their charging horses to a halt.

Cassandra stared at Charles, not at a loss for words but finding the ones that occurred completely unacceptable. "I love you," for example, was unthinkable, let alone fit to be uttered aloud now.

The problem was that Charles Danforth was confusing her by saying nothing, just looking at her as if she were one of the wonders of the world. She reached up to tuck her straying hair underneath her hat.

He grinned suddenly. "No need for that. The word's out. I know that you're a woman."

She reddened a bit for her past follies. "What are you doing here, Captain Danforth?" She managed a near-normal tone.

"Oh, I would have been here a lot sooner, but first I had to spend some time in London with my father. By the by, the old man's not half bad when you get to know him. Wants me to take over the hall when I marry. Says he actually prefers the Dower House.

"Then, after that, it took me two days to get Trafalgar

back. The curst fellow I sold him to didn't want to part with him.''

"You sold Trafalgar?'' Cassandra suddenly lost her self-consciousness and looked at him with horror.

"Knew that wouldn't set too well with you. But what else was I to do? I couldn't go to France. Not now.''

"But to sell Trafalgar!''

"No need trying to make me feel like a criminal. I tell you, I had no other choice.''

"Oh, yes, you did,'' she said bitterly. "My father gave you one. I heard him.''

"The devil you did!'' He groaned. "Of all the rotten luck. Your father, begging your pardon, Cassie, is a chuckle-head. Thinking he could bribe me into a marriage.''

"He meant well, I suppose.'' She couldn't look at him.

"Maybe so. But he couldn't have made a bigger botch of things if he'd practiced. Can you imagine what our marriage would have been like with you thinking I'd been bought?''

Cassandra remained silent, not about to let her mind wander through such musings.

"Pure hell,'' he answered for her. "That's why I had to pay off Grimes myself. And since Trafalgar was all I owned of value, I sold him. But with the option to buy him back. Then the blackguard wouldn't sell!

"I tell you, Cassie, my faith in my fellow man has been sorely tried here lately. I even explained to the cove that the horse was to be my dowry, so to speak. Told him that the woman I intend to marry wants to start a horse farm and actually prefers the animal to me. Do you know, he didn't find that nearly as hard to believe as I would have hoped.'' He grinned as she stared at him. "But, anyhow, after some persuasion that ended in blows, he finally did agree to stake the horse at cards. And, lord, was he a sharper! Took me thirty-six hours to win Trafalgar back. But, anyway, here we are at last. By the by, your father said you were in love with me. Was he right?''

She flushed but managed to look at him steadily. "Why should I be any different from every other female you meet?''

"Well,'' he said as he dismounted, "since you are, actually, very different in most respects from every other female that I've met, it did occur to me you might be in this case, too.''

He reached up, lifted her from her horse, and held her tight, gazing down into her eyes, his heart reflected in his own. His lips met hers, lightly at first, then with a hungry intensity. The kiss went on and on, while Trafalgar and Pegasus shook their manes impatiently, longing to resume their gallop. Finally, mystified by such odd human behavior, they wandered off toward a nearby stream.

Some moments later, Charles and Cassandra, both now suffering from an acute weakness of the knees, sank down on the grass beneath a tree, where he put his arms about her and she nestled back against his shoulder.

''Well, we've settled that point at least,'' he murmured with satisfaction.

''Which point is that?''

''Whether or not you love me.''

She glared up at him indignantly. ''That was never at issue, you ninnyhammer. The real question, Casanova, is whether you love me.''

''Love you!'' He glared back. ''Didn't I sell Trafalgar? What better proof could you ask of me than that?''

The argument was sound. Cassandra raised her lips to meet his kiss again.

''What do you say to Ireland for our wedding trip?'' he asked at the next interval.

''Ireland?'' She sounded surprised.

''Yes. It was my father's notion, actually. But I'll have to admit I think it's a capital idea. Best place in the world to buy breeding stock.''

''Well,'' she replied thoughtfully, ''I don't know. I did rather have my heart set on France.''

''France!''

''Just funning, love.''

Lady Cassandra Devenham stopped Captain the Honorable Charles Danforth's howl of protest with her lips.

True romance is <u>not</u> hard to find... you need only look as far as FAWCETT BOOKS